PERIL IN LITTLE LEAF CREEK

A LITTLE LEAF CREEK COZY MYSTERY

CINDY BELL

CONTENTS

Chapter 1	1
Chapter 2	12
Chapter 3	23
Chapter 4	31
Chapter 5	38
Chapter 6	46
Chapter 7	55
Chapter 8	67
Chapter 9	74
Chapter 10	82
Chapter 11	90
Chapter 12	97
Chapter 13	104
Chapter 14	112
Chapter 15	118
Chapter 16	126
Chapter 17	137
Chapter 18	144
Chapter 19	152
Chapter 20	158
Chapter 21	166
Chapter 22	173
Chapter 23	181
Chapter 24	188
Chapter 25	196
Chapter 26	209

About the Author	217
Also by Cindy Bell	219
Tessa's Baked Strawberry Cheesecake Recipe	225

Copyright © 2020 Cindy Bell
All rights reserved.

Cover Design by Lou Harper, Cover Affairs

All rights reserved. No part of this publication may be reproduced or transmitted in any form or by any means, electronic or mechanical, including photocopy, recording, or any information storage or retrieval system, without permission in writing from the publisher.

This is a work of fiction. The characters, incidents and locations portrayed in this book and the names herein are fictitious. Any similarity to or identification with the locations, names, characters or history of any person, product or entity is entirely coincidental and unintentional.

All trademarks and brands referred to in this book are for illustrative purposes only, are the property of their respective owners and not affiliated with this publication in any way. Any trademarks are being used without permission, and the publication of the trademark is not authorized by, associated with or sponsored by the trademark owner.

ISBN: 9798675483273

CHAPTER 1

"Higher." Sebastian Vail grunted as he eased the piece of wood up against the ceiling. His arms flexed under his rolled up sleeves, as he added pressure.

"Like this?" Cassie Alberta blew a strand of hair away from her eyes as she struggled to hold the wood above her head. She raised up on her toes and tightened her muscles, hoping not to lose her balance.

"Perfect," Sebastian replied in his smooth accent.

Do not be distracted, Cassie. She squeezed her eyes shut and focused on keeping the board in the air as she heard the drill whir to life. What had started as a simple patch in the ceiling, had turned into a crown molding project, thanks to Sebastian's know-how, and insistence. She wondered if he had ever done anything simple in his life, or if he always went for spectacular.

"Alright, nice and easy, let go," Sebastian murmured, as if speaking too loud might cause the entire ceiling to cave in.

As Cassie slowly pulled her fingers away they trembled, both from exertion, and from nervousness. After purchasing a fixer-upper, a two-story farmhouse in Little Leaf Creek, Sebastian, who owned a farm that backed up to her property, had practically taken over her repair plans. She didn't mind, but she still wasn't sure how to take him. He pushed his blond hair back behind his ears and flashed her a wide smile.

"Pretty, right?"

"So pretty." Cassie gazed into his warm brown eyes for a long moment, then blinked and looked up at the molding. "I mean, I'm sure it will be, once we get it painted."

"Did you look at those color swatches I brought over?" Sebastian pulled a dark blue bandanna out of his back pocket and used it to wipe the sweat off of the back of his neck. He jumped down from the table they'd both been standing on in order to reach the ceiling, and offered his hand to her to help her down.

Cassie eased her way off the table and pretended not to notice the way her mind spun as his fingers curled around hers.

"Actually, I haven't had a chance, yet." Cassie's heart skipped a beat as he glanced over at her. Was that disappointment she saw in his eyes? "I'm still unpacking, and I've taken on some more shifts at Mirabel's, so it's been a bit of a juggling act."

"Right, no rush." Sebastian tucked the bandanna into his back pocket again, then swept his gaze along the ceiling. "I think you're really going to like it when it's done." He placed his hands on his hips and leaned back some as he surveyed their work.

"Cassie!" Someone called her name as the front door swung open. "Cassie, are you home?"

Cassie recognized the voice this time. It belonged to Detective Oliver Graham.

"Oliver, what are you doing here?" Cassie smiled.

"Oh, I'm going door to door, just notifying the residents on this street about an incident." Oliver's words slowed as his gaze settled on Sebastian. "Sebastian."

"Detective." Sebastian pulled his baseball cap on

over his blond hair, then narrowed his eyes. "What incident?"

"There was a burglary in Freemar, and the police there think the two suspects probably fled in this direction. Maybe headed into the woods and even up to the cliffs. Since your farm has direct access to the woods, and Cassie's backyard backs onto your farm, I figured this might be the area they would head for." Oliver shifted his gaze back to Cassie, his sharp gray eyes met hers. "You'll want to make sure that you keep things locked up, at least for the next few days."

"Are you sure they're around here?" Cassie frowned at the thought. She'd moved from the big city to a small town and expected things to be a little slower, as things had been during the years she had grown up in an even smaller town. So far that hadn't been the case. If anything, everything moved fast in Little Leaf Creek. Good news, bad news, and gossip, traveled at the speed of light.

At the first sign of a violation, the historical society snapped into action. The police were called for everything from bikes piled up outside of the corner store, to ducks blocking the roads. Town hall meetings were called regularly to ensure that the community knew about the rules in place and could vote on new rules being introduced. The people in Little Leaf Creek were quick to react, and to judge. So far she hadn't exactly been accepted with open arms by everyone into their community.

"If I was sure, they'd be in handcuffs." Oliver smiled.

"So, you're really telling every resident on this street, in person?" Sebastian tipped his cap up some as he looked at Oliver. "That's quite kind of you to go out of your way, when you could easily make a call or send a text."

"I figured Cassie might be home." Oliver shrugged as he glanced at Sebastian. "I wanted to make sure she was safe, since she lives alone."

"She's safe." Sebastian's lips spread into a full smile, one that didn't reach his eyes, or the tone of his voice.

"Thanks for coming by, Oliver." Cassie walked toward the kitchen. "Let me get you a drink before you head out. It's hot out there, you must be thirsty."

"Thanks Cassie." Oliver smiled.

"I'll grab you a glass of lemonade, too, Sebastian." Cassie focused on finding clean glasses, and poured three servings of the lemonade she'd made that morning. In her old life, she bought fresh squeezed lemonade, she didn't make it herself. In her old life, she didn't often have guests just pop in. A twinge of guilt rippled through her as she realized that her heart still pounded swiftly. Why? Why did she get stirred up by either of them? She had no right to even think about being attracted to another man. Not after her husband had died, not even a year before.

Get it together, Cassie. She took a deep breath as she tucked one of the glasses between her forearm and her chest, and held the other two in her hands. These men aren't the least bit interested in you, and fooling yourself into thinking that they are is only going to make your life harder.

Cassie returned to the living room and found that Sebastian and Oliver had stepped out onto the front porch.

Cassie nudged her way through the screen door and out onto the porch as well.

"Oh, let me get that." Sebastian plucked the glass from her hand.

Cassie held out one of the glasses to Oliver.

"I guess you have your work cut out for you then?"

"I do." Oliver took the glass as he met her eyes. "Thank you for this." He took a sip, then glanced away as his lips puckered.

"A bit too tart?" Cassie frowned as she recalled her nearly hour long debate about whether to add more sugar.

"It's perfect." Oliver licked his lips. "Sebastian, since your property has so many outbuildings, it would help me out a lot if you could keep an eye on them. Keep the barn locked up. At least until I get my hands on these two."

"Is it kids you're hunting?" Sebastian leaned against the railing of the porch and swallowed a mouthful of lemonade.

Cassie noticed his eyes crinkle as he swallowed.

"Quite a kick there, Cassie." Sebastian winked at her. "It's not every girl that can handle a strong lemonade."

"It was my first try." Cassie winced. Girl? She was closing in on forty, and the thirty-seven year old man, who could have passed for being in his twenties, called her 'girl'. He always seemed to be teasing her. "I might need a little more time to get the hang of it."

"I'm happy to test it out along the way." Sebastian's eyes lingered on hers for a moment before he looked over at Oliver. "So? Is it a couple of kids? I mean, is it really that big of a deal if they grabbed a few bags of chips?"

"It was an armed robbery." Oliver's tone hardened slightly as he turned to face Sebastian. "I'm sure you don't want a couple of kids running around your property with a gun they don't know how to use. It's serious. Besides, one is nineteen, one is twenty. They're not kids."

"Might as well be." Cassie took a sip from her own glass. Yes, pure sour. She had forgotten to stir it up before she poured it. "But a gun in the wrong hands is always dangerous."

"Just do me a favor and keep an eye on your outbuildings, alright?" Oliver shook his head. "The sooner we get these two behind bars, the safer everyone will be."

Cassie caught sight of her neighbor, Tessa Watters, as she opened her door to let her dog, Harry, out into the yard. Harry bolted toward the fence and barked at the three gathered on the porch. Cassie raised her hand to wave to Tessa who gave a quick wave, then pulled the door shut. She glanced over at Oliver, who turned away, as if he hadn't seen Tessa, though she was certain that he had.

"Are you ever going to tell me what really happened between the two of you?" Cassie crossed her arms as she stared at Oliver's back.

"Nothing more to say about it." Oliver cleared his

throat as he turned back to face her. He reached into his pocket and pulled out a dog treat, then tossed it across the side yard and fence, right into Harry's mouth.

The dog bounded back and forth along the fence, clearly overjoyed. The goats, Billy and Gerry, in the large backyard cast lazy stares at the dog, then returned to nibbling on the shrubs.

"Good boy, Harry." Oliver smiled. Not the strained expression that Cassie had come to recognize as perpetual tension in the man's muscles, but a full, relaxed, and warm smile. Concentrating on it for just a moment, she didn't hear what Sebastian said.

"What was that?" Cassie looked over at him.

"I just said, I'll be sure to check on the buildings." Sebastian met her eyes, then took another sip of his lemonade.

"Great, thanks." Oliver drew her attention back to him.

"It looks like Harry is a big fan of yours." Cassie smiled as the collie mix jumped up against the fence and gave Oliver a friendly bark.

"He's a good pooch." Oliver tossed him another treat.

"I guess you two were pretty close. As close as

you and Tessa were." Cassie tipped her head to the side as she scrutinized his expression. "What changed that?"

"It's in the past." Oliver settled his eyes on hers.

"I just hate to see two people who obviously used to be friends and care about each other, kept apart by some silly grudge. Maybe if you told me about it, I could help." Cassie smiled.

"Well, that works both ways. When you want to talk about what happened with your husband, I'm all ears." Oliver's jaw rippled.

"Oliver!" Sebastian set his glass down hard on the porch railing.

"All I'm saying is you don't have to carry it alone, you know. Maybe there's something I can do to help." Oliver searched her eyes.

"Stop." Cassie took a step back. "Please." She wasn't ready to talk about her husband's sudden death.

"I'm sorry." Oliver glanced away from her. "I didn't mean to upset you."

"It's okay." Cassie smiled slightly, as she tried to reassure him. "I just don't want to talk about it."

"I think you better hurry and go and catch those criminals before they get away." Sebastian shifted closer to Cassie as he fixed his gaze on Oliver.

Cassie's cheeks burned from the shock of Oliver talking about her late husband. Oliver was a difficult man to read. One moment she thought he was kind and determined, the next she saw him as callous and obsessive.

"I'll be on my way." Oliver ran his hand back through his neatly trimmed dark hair and glanced over at Cassie. "If you ever want to talk about it, I'm here." He turned and walked down the steps of the porch.

"Thank you." Cassie called out to him.

Sebastian took a step toward Cassie.

"Are you okay?"

"I'm fine." Cassie didn't want to talk about her history. She wanted to leave it in the past. After all, that was one of the reasons she had moved to Little Leaf Creek.

CHAPTER 2

"Trevor!" Sebastian called out.

Cassie followed Sebastian's gaze toward the street and saw Trevor Danel, a local artist who had created a beautiful statue out of harvested scrap metal, which now resided in the center of her front yard.

"Sebastian." Trevor stopped on the sidewalk. "Did you hear about Clyde?"

"What about him?" Sebastian took a step closer to him.

"Hi Trevor." Cassie waved him toward the porch. Although they had their disagreements, when someone was found murdered on her front lawn on the first day she moved into Little Leaf Creek, they were slowly putting that in the past and becoming friends.

"I'll show you." Trevor looked at Sebastian. "Wait until you see this." He ran up the steps of the front porch and whipped out a tablet from one of the deep pockets of his over-sized jacket. Barely in his twenties, Trevor still carried the exuberance of adolescence while trying to forge his way into adulthood.

Cassie could see how he must have looked as a young child, bubbling over with excitement, as he looked at Sebastian eagerly and held up the tablet.

"Here, I'll show you." Trevor pressed the play button on the screen and handed it to Sebastian, then looked at Cassie. "One of the best climbers in the whole state is about to spend some time on our mountain. Watch!"

Sebastian held onto the small tablet as Cassie and Trevor stood close to him and watched the video play.

A man who looked to be in his thirties appeared on the screen, with a man closer to Trevor's age right beside him.

"I am so jealous of Aiden!" Trevor groaned. "I wish it was me going camping and climbing with Clyde. But I'm not much of a climber." He shrugged.

In the video, the two men bantered back and forth about their plan to go rock climbing in an area that was generally not explored by most. Clyde listed the dangers they might face, while Aiden joked about wrestling a mountain lion with his bare hands.

"That was a house cat, and you hid in the tent while it ate your fish!" Clyde gave Aiden a hard clap on his back as they both burst out laughing.

"Isn't he great?" Trevor grinned as he stared at Clyde. "He taught me so much when I was a kid. I wasn't really into camping, but he still made sure that I learned."

"He sure has a lot of enthusiasm." Cassie glanced up from the tablet and smiled at Trevor. "He must mean a lot to you."

"He does." Trevor looked at her. "The last time I saw my dad, when he made one of his rare visits to town, Clyde called him out for walking out on my mother. They all went to high school together." He shrugged. "It was about ten years ago, but it still sticks out in my mind. I'd never seen anyone stand up to my dad before, but Clyde wouldn't back down. He didn't have to do that, but he did it anyway."

"He's a decent fellow." Sebastian nodded, as the video came to an end. "I hear he's going to open a business with Shane Carlo. They want to become some kind of tourist magnet for rock climbing and adventure trips."

"That would be amazing!" Trevor took a deep breath. "But he's still not getting me on that mountain, no way."

"What's so wrong with the mountain?" Cassie raised her eyebrows as she smiled at Trevor.

"Well, besides the fact that I am not fond of heights and rock climbing. Bugs." Trevor scrunched up his nose. "This big!" He held his hands wide apart from each other.

"Oh, it can't be that bad." Cassie laughed as she watched him playfully swat his hands through the air.

"Oh yeah? When was the last time you went camping?" Trevor smiled.

"It's been a long time." Cassie's voice softened as she recalled a few star-filled nights she'd spent at summer camp as a child. It seemed like a lifetime ago.

"We could go sometime." Sebastian leaned up against the railing beside her. "I'll protect you from the bugs."

Cassie briefly looked into his eyes and wondered about the warmth she read there. Was he laughing at her?

"I'm sure you have plenty of better things to do." She grinned at him, then looked back at Trevor. "But I'll go if you go, Trevor."

"That's a big nope." Trevor shook his head as he backed away from the two of them. "Zero interest in getting any form of itchy rash. You know that plants can actually attack you?" He frowned. "Do your research, that's all I'm saying."

"I'll make sure I do that." Cassie grinned, as she nudged him with her elbow. "But I bet there are scarier things than a few creepy-crawlies."

"Maybe, but I don't want to find out." Trevor tugged his phone from his pocket, checked a message, then started toward the steps of the porch. "Going to go see him off. Later guys!" He waved to them as he pounded down the stairs.

"I miss those days, being that excited." Cassie glanced over at Sebastian. "Do you?"

"I still have them." Sebastian met her eyes, then angled the brim of his cap a little lower over his face. "I'd better go check those outbuildings as the detective suggested. Make sure you lock up."

"Thanks for all your help, Sebastian. Let me get my checkbook." Cassie turned toward the front door of the house, but his long fingers that wrapped around her wrist, stopped her.

"I'm not taking any money from you, Cassie." Sebastian released her hand as she turned back to face him.

"That's kind of you, Sebastian, but you've spent so much time helping me, I need to pay you something." Cassie frowned as she crossed her arms.

"Your company is plenty." Sebastian stepped down off the porch.

"It's not nearly enough." Cassie followed after him, determined to get her point across. "Sebastian, please, I don't want to feel like I'm taking advantage of you."

Sebastian reached the gate, then looked back at her.

"I've told you before. That's not how things work around here, Cassie. You may be used to everything being about money, but here, it's about community. At least, it is to me."

"But I have the money to pay you. I have the money." Cassie sputtered out her words. They fell heavily on her ears as she spoke them, each one sounding more and more petty to her.

"Good to know." Sebastian nodded to her, then pushed through the gate and walked off.

Cassie's heart sank as she wondered if she'd just offended him, and changed his impression of her.

She spent the rest of the day working on the house. Every time she finished one chore, she noticed three others that needed to be done. But it didn't feel like a burden to her. She felt as if she finally had a place of her own. A place that didn't harbor old memories, a place that could be carved out to represent her, and no one else.

By the time Cassie sprawled out in bed that night, her muscles ached, as did her heart. As much as she wanted to start her new life, there were things about her old life that she still hadn't been able to let go of, and Oliver had stirred that up for her that day. She squeezed her eyes shut and forced the thoughts away.

What felt like moments later, Cassie's alarm sounded, summoning her to get up as she had to go to Mirabel's Diner for the early morning shift.

After getting ready Cassie drove to the diner. She opened the door to the diner and stepped into the intoxicating aroma of freshly brewed coffee and cinnamon rolls baking in the kitchen. As she took a deep breath, a smile settled on her lips. She'd trade all of the luxury she'd experienced in her adult life, for that one moment, that one experience.

"Cassie!" Mirabel Light rounded the counter and threw her arms around her in a warm hug. "So good to see you this morning."

"It is?" Cassie smiled, dumbfounded, as the other woman stepped away from her.

"Sure."

"Is there something special about today?"

"Every day is special with you here." Mirabel grinned. "Let's make sure we have a wonderful day."

"Okay." Cassie laughed, as she grabbed her apron from the hook next to the kitchen doors. "What's gotten into you today?"

"Can't I just be happy?" Mirabel flicked her long, red braid over her shoulder, then raised her eyebrows. "It's not illegal, you know?"

"Of course not." Cassie walked up beside her. "I'm glad you're happy. You're almost always happy. You just seem happier than usual."

"It's going to be a great day." Mirabel took a deep breath. "I can feel it."

The front door of the diner swung open and a group of five people stepped inside, chatting away.

"I saw all of the flashing lights first thing this morning, even before I got the paper." The man in the front of the group shook his head as he approached one of the large tables in the middle of the diner. "It has to be something big for that many rescue vehicles to be going up there."

"What do you think it is?" A woman sat down across from him. "A mudslide?"

"It hasn't been raining enough for that." The man that sat down beside her shook his head. "Maybe someone got lost in the woods?"

"I heard that the police have been hunting a couple of burglars from Freemar." The youngest woman of the group sat down at the table. "I bet that's what it's all about."

"Maybe, but they were rescue vehicles." The woman who sat on the other side of her shook her head. "I don't think they would use rescue vehicles in a hunt for criminals."

"Unless someone got hurt in the process." The first man held up one finger. "I bet that's what happened."

"Listen to this crew." Mirabel smiled as she walked over to them with Cassie at her side. "Buzzing already this morning, are you?"

"Didn't you hear the sirens?" The youngest woman met Mirabel's eyes.

"Can't say I did, Sally. I must have already been

here." Mirabel glanced over at Cassie. "Did you hear anything?"

"No, nothing."

"Well, then you missed it." Sally shook her head. "It was so loud I thought there must be a fire or something." She looked at the woman beside her. "It woke us both up didn't it, Heather?"

"Yes." Heather covered her mouth as she yawned. "And I'd rather be back in bed. But now I have to know what's going on."

"Anything on the town page about it?" Mirabel squinted as she tried to peer at Sally's phone.

"Nothing yet. Just a lot of people talking about the sirens, but no news on why." Sally looked up and straight into Cassie's eyes. "Why don't you ask Ollie?"

"Me?" Cassie laughed as she shook her head. "I can't do that."

"I saw him at your house yesterday." The first man who sat down grinned.

"Cool it, Cooper." Mirabel crossed her arms. "That is nothing to concern you."

Cassie marveled at the fact that the stranger knew about people coming and going from her house. This really was a small town.

"Sorry, but I think you have the wrong

impression." Cassie looked toward the door as another group of people stepped inside.

Cassie walked toward them, ready to show them to a table and take their order. But before she could, a ripple of excitement broke out among them.

"My wife will let us know what's going on, she's one of the paramedics." A man at the front of the crowd pulled his phone from his pocket. His eyes widened as he looked at the screen. "It's Clyde!" He spoke up, probably louder than he intended. "It's Clyde, he died by the cliffs!"

CHAPTER 3

*C*assie sucked down a sharp breath as she recognized the name. She doubted that two Clydes had been rock climbing on the same day. Her thoughts shifted to Trevor, and how he would take the news.

"You can't be serious!" Cooper leaned forward. "Are you sure about that, Scott, or is it just a rumor?"

"You know my wife is a paramedic. She's by the cliffs now." Scott frowned as he shoved his phone back into his pocket. "She wouldn't make something like that up."

"Of course she wouldn't, Scott." Mirabel's voice was soothing, but firm at the same time. "I know we all love to keep abreast of what's going on in our town, but the truth is, we're better off waiting for the real details from the proper authorities."

Everyone fell silent for a few moments, then Sally looked up from her phone.

"They're calling it an accident! He left a gas stove on inside of his tent!"

"Well, it was a nice idea while it lasted." Mirabel shook her head, then began to take orders.

Cassie did the same, though it was hard for her to concentrate. From what Trevor had told her about Clyde, she doubted that the man could have made such a foolish mistake. He'd camped hundreds if not thousands of times. Had he had a bit too much to drink and passed out? But why would the stove be in his tent? She considered the possibilities as she took orders from more and more customers. The door just kept swinging open. The conversations spanned from table to table, including the booths on the sidewalls.

"It feels like one big community meeting out there." Cassie sighed as she stepped behind the front counter.

"Everyone is pretty worked up about this. Clyde was a popular guy, and not just here, he was pretty well known thanks to all of the videos he posted online." Mirabel crossed her arms as she leaned back against the wall and looked out at the crowded diner. "Lots of people aren't buying this story about the way he died either."

"Well, he had his friend up there with him, right? Aiden? He should know what happened to him." Cassie picked up a bottle of ketchup to deliver to one of the tables.

"Aiden?" Mirabel's blue eyes widened as she stared at Cassie. "He had Aiden with him?"

"According to the video he posted yesterday, yes." Cassie frowned. "Do you know him?"

"Oh no! I have to call June! I had no idea Aiden was supposed to be with him!" Mirabel grabbed her cell phone from the back counter and ran toward the kitchen. "I need a few minutes, Cassie!"

Cassie stared after her, startled by her state of panic. Then she jumped at the sound of someone calling for her attention. As she turned back to the sea of faces in the dining room, she realized that she was quite outnumbered.

As Cassie did her best to keep up with the demands of the customers, she felt a bit winded. Sometimes it took a little convincing for her to believe that she was nearing forty, other times she was very aware. This was one of those times. She tried to catch her breath as she waited for an order to come up.

Mirabel brushed past her with tears in her eyes.

"Mirabel?" Cassie followed after her. "What's wrong? Are you okay?"

"No, I'm not." Mirabel gulped back a sob as she grabbed her purse from under the counter. "My good friend, June, can't find her son. Aiden, he's like a nephew to me. She thought he was going rock climbing with Clyde, but no one has been able to find him. She's worried sick that something happened to him, too. I'm so sorry, Cassie, I hate to do this to you, but I have to go be with her. I've called in some help, they should be here soon."

"It's okay, I understand. Go be with her. I hope Aiden turns up soon, perfectly healthy." Cassie's chest tightened at the thought of the young man in the woods alone, possibly injured.

"Me too!" Mirabel hurried out the door. As she passed through it, she nearly bumped into a woman who stepped inside. She glanced over her shoulder at Mirabel, then settled her eyes on Cassie.

"Tessa?" Cassie blinked in disbelief. Tessa rarely showed her face in the diner, she preferred to keep to herself. In fact, Cassie didn't think she had ever seen Tessa in the diner.

"Cassie." Tessa walked toward the front counter as Frankie, the cook, rang the bell in the kitchen.

"Give me a few minutes, Tessa, I've got to get these orders out." Cassie's heart pounded as she ran the orders from table to table. She refilled drinks, patted shoulders, and brought out extra cream for coffee. When she returned to the counter, Tessa leaned on the counter.

"Are you all alone here?"

"For the moment, there are more people coming in soon. Can I get you some coffee?" Cassie grabbed the pot behind her and filled a mug before Tessa could answer.

"Did you hear what happened?" Tessa frowned as she took a sip of the black coffee.

"Yes, it's all I've been hearing about." Cassie ran her gaze over the dining room in search of any hands waving in the air, then she looked back at Tessa. "It's such a tragic accident."

"Oh no, Cassie." Tessa cleared her throat as she narrowed her eyes. "It's not a tragic accident, it's a murder."

"What?" Cassie's heart skipped a beat. Even though she already had her doubts that it could be an accident, hearing Tessa confirm what she was thinking shocked her. "How can you be sure?"

"I can be sure because I know Clyde Timpson, and I know that he would never have put that stove inside his tent." Tessa shook her head. "There's no way."

"Things happen, Tessa. Maybe he fell asleep, or maybe he was drinking, or using drugs. Maybe he just didn't think about it. We all make mistakes sometimes." Cassie frowned as she spotted a customer waving goodbye to her. She smiled and waved in return.

"He would never take the stove into his tent, let alone leave it on. Not Clyde, he would never make a mistake like that. Not when it came to climbing, or camping. He's had years of experience. He rescued more climbers than anyone else I know." Tessa sighed and closed her eyes.

"I'm sorry, Tessa, I didn't know you knew him so well." Cassie put her hand on her shoulder and squeezed it. "I'm very sorry for your loss."

"I didn't know him well. We ran into each other a few times over the years. We'd spoken a few times. He helped me on a couple of investigations." Tessa lowered her eyes. "We weren't friends, but I respected him as a professional, and I'll tell you this, if he knew what people were saying about how he died, he would be furious."

Cassie chewed on her bottom lip as she wondered if she should point out again, that everyone made mistakes. Tessa wasn't the type to argue with. She was almost always one hundred percent confident in whatever she said. And Cassie already had her doubts about it being an accident.

"I'll be right back to talk with you about it. I just need to see if anyone needs anything." Cassie stepped away from her. "Don't go anywhere!"

The door swung open and a few more people stepped inside.

"Getting a bit crowded in here for me." Tessa winced, then took a big swallow of her coffee.

Cassie felt a wave of relief as she recognized two other waitresses that came in with the crowd. She summoned their help as soon as they had their aprons on. From the strange looks they gave her, she knew they didn't enjoy being ordered around by the 'new girl'. Despite being twice their age, and the several weeks that had passed since she began working there, she guessed that she would always be the 'new girl'.

Just as Cassie finished her rounds with the diners, she heard the door swing open again. She turned to look, uncertain whether there would be anywhere to seat another wave of customers, and found Trevor in the doorway. His clothes were soaked from head to toe, she guessed from the rain that had begun to fall outside. He glared at the entire gathering, then in a loud voice called out.

"It's not true! None of it!"

CHAPTER 4

"Trevor!" Cassie walked toward him as a few shouts escalated the tension in the diner.

"It's not true!" Trevor looked around the crowd. "I am going to find out exactly what happened to Clyde, I won't rest until I find out, and whoever did it is going to pay!"

"Enough." Cooper stood up from his table. "Don't be coming in here shouting and carrying on. Get out of here with that nonsense."

"I'm not going anywhere!" Trevor's hands whipped through the air and accidently knocked off the hat of a man seated near him.

That man shot up from the table and lunged toward Trevor.

"Stop!" Cassie called out. "Listen everyone, I know that tensions are running high. None of us expected this to happen. People loved Clyde very much, and there are going to be feelings of anger and grief. Please, everyone just calm down."

"Why don't you tell him that?" The man glared at Trevor.

"I'm trying to." Cassie frowned as she walked up to Trevor, whose face was red from anger. "Trevor, come over here and talk to me about all of this. I know you're upset."

"Upset?" Trevor gripped his hands into fists. "You have no idea what I'm feeling! Someone killed him!"

"It was an accident." A man called out from the middle of the diner.

"It wasn't!" Trevor turned toward the man.

"That's enough, Trevor, come sit down." Cassie steered him toward the front counter.

"Cassie, you have no idea what's going on here." Trevor growled his words.

"You need to calm down, Trevor." Tessa stepped up beside Cassie.

"What's going on here?" Oliver's hands settled on Trevor's shoulders as he stepped up behind him. "You're causing quite a scene here, Trevor, and I'd hate to be the one that has to call your mother to bail you out of jail."

"I didn't do anything!" Trevor spun around to face Oliver who took a quick step back.

"Easy there." Oliver narrowed his eyes. His voice hardened as he spoke again. "You've got three seconds to sit down on one of those stools before you're in handcuffs."

"Trevor." Cassie grabbed his hand. "Please, just listen." Her heart raced as she wondered if Oliver would really arrest him. She guessed that he would, since he appeared to be a by-the-book detective that didn't take non-compliance lightly. "I'll get you a milkshake." Her words sounded absurd even to her own ears as she coaxed Trevor toward the counter.

"Chocolate?" Trevor sighed as he slumped down on the stool.

"Absolutely." Cassie frowned, as she watched Oliver step up right behind Trevor.

"Detective, can I get you anything?" Cassie noticed the other patrons in the diner kept a close eye on her, and Oliver.

"Detective?" Oliver eyed her for a moment. "I'll take a cup of coffee please."

Tessa eased down onto the barstool beside

Trevor. She picked up her cup of coffee and took a sip, as if nothing had happened.

"You're going to drink coffee instead of looking for Clyde's killer?" Trevor glared at Oliver.

"Right now, his death is classified as an accident." Oliver's voice softened as he turned to look at Trevor. "We are still evaluating the circumstances surrounding his death. I know that you're upset, Trevor, but you're going to have to give us a little time to investigate. Actually, you can help me with that."

"I'll do anything I can to help." Trevor spoke slowly, his voice laced with skepticism as he stared at Oliver.

"When was the last time you heard from your father, Trevor?" Oliver set his coffee cup down on the counter and focused his attention on the younger man.

"My father?" Trevor frowned. "Why would you ask me about him?"

"Just answer the question, please. Have you been in contact with him recently?"

Cassie stepped closer as she noted a shift in Oliver's tone and expression. He exuded authority as he straightened his shoulders and narrowed his eyes.

"I don't hear from my dad. We're not in contact

with each other. I haven't seen him in over ten years. As far as I know he's dead. That's what we presume anyway. If you were any kind of detective, you would know that already." Trevor scoffed as he turned to the chocolate milkshake that Cassie set down in front of him.

"Did you know he is in town?" Oliver straightened his shoulders.

Cassie felt on edge by Oliver's demeanor. She looked over at Tessa, who only shook her head.

"He's here? I said I don't hear from him!" Trevor looked at Oliver.

"Are you sure?" Oliver spoke in a milder tone. "You said you wanted to help with the case, I'm just asking you whether you saw or spoke to your father in the past day or so."

"Of course not." Trevor crossed his arms. "I thought he was probably dead. He knows better than to speak to me." He paused, then tilted his head to the side. "Are you saying he's really here?"

"I'm not saying anything for certain at the moment. But that's what I've heard." Oliver finished the last sip of his coffee, then set some cash down on the counter. "I'm just trying to figure out exactly what happened at the campsite."

"I can tell you what didn't." Trevor shook his

head. "Clyde didn't leave that stove on inside of his tent. Someone killed him."

"As of now, we are investigating an accidental death. But if you happen to run into your father, please contact me." Oliver glanced over at Cassie with a slight nod.

"That's nonsense." Trevor jumped to his feet, though he was careful to keep his distance from Oliver. "It wasn't an accident! You need to do your job and find out what happened to him!"

"I'm going to do just that." Oliver locked his eyes to Trevor's. "So, do me a favor and make sure I don't get pulled away because some kid is throwing a tantrum in the middle of a diner, alright?"

"I'm an adult." Trevor huffed as he stared at Oliver in disbelief.

"Then act like it." Oliver turned and walked toward the door of the diner.

Tessa stood up and caught him by the arm before he could make his way through it.

Oliver tensed, but stopped.

Cassie noticed the way he turned slowly to face Tessa, wielding none of the authority that he'd just shown Trevor. As she stepped around the counter to console the young man, she saw Tessa and Oliver lock eyes.

"You know better than to think this was an accident, Ollie." Tessa stepped closer to Oliver.

"I know that I will follow wherever the evidence leads me." Oliver turned and walked out the door.

CHAPTER 5

Tessa made her way back to the counter, her faint limp pronounced with each step she took.

"Are you okay, Tessa?" Cassie looked over at her as she reached her side.

"I will be, when that kid gets his head out of the sand." Tessa rolled her eyes.

"Tessa." Cassie watched Oliver's car drive past the front window of the diner. "He's just trying to do his job."

"Letter of the law, right?" Tessa smiled.

Cassie wanted to ask Tessa more about her relationship with Oliver. She couldn't deny the fact that she was extremely curious about him and his history with Tessa, but whenever she asked either of them about it they were evasive.

"I can't believe my dad is in town. It's just like him to come into town after ten years and not say a word about it to me or my mom." Trevor shook his head as he headed for the door. "I'd better go check on my mom, he's always trying to give her a hard time about things."

"Be careful, Trevor." Cassie frowned as she watched him disappear through the door. She shifted her attention to Tessa, who gazed down into her nearly empty cup.

"So, you don't think this was an accident, Tessa?" Cassie leaned against the counter as she looked up at her.

"There is no way this was an accident." Tessa clasped her hands together on the counter. "Someone killed Clyde. But if Oliver isn't convinced, it's probably because there's no proof that he was murdered."

"It's possible that someone staged his death, to make it look like an accident, isn't it?" Cassie walked over to a nearby table to freshen up their coffee. When she returned, Tessa placed some money on the counter.

"It's definitely possible, but without some kind of

evidence, it's not going to matter. I would never believe that he would have that stove in his tent, but I can't prove that." Tessa stood up from the stool. "I'm going to take Harry to the campsite, and have a good look around."

"Do you think that's a good idea?" Cassie winced. "If someone did kill Clyde, what if the killer is still around there?"

"Oh, trust me, no one is going to waste their time on killing this old fool." Tessa winked as she walked toward the door.

Tessa stepped out, just as Mirabel stepped in. She glanced around at the nearly empty diner and walked up to Cassie.

"What happened here?"

"Oliver." Cassie raised her eyebrows. "Or more specifically, Trevor and Oliver. Trevor was upset about Clyde and got into a bit of an argument with Oliver and a lot of people decided to leave." She looked into her friend's eyes. "How are you? How's June? Any news on Aiden?"

"She's a mess." Mirabel sighed and stepped behind the counter. "Unfortunately, we haven't heard anything new about Aiden. At this point we're just hoping that he's alright. But his mother is worried sick. So am I."

"You shouldn't be here. I can stay as long as you need."

"No, actually, you should go home and rest. It's been a crazy morning and I know you handled a crowd on your own. Right now, we don't know anything. If something does come up, I'm going to need to leave to be with June. So, it's best if you're rested up in case that happens." Mirabel wiped a hand across her forehead and frowned. "It's going to be quiet for a while now, anyway, until the next tidbit of news is released."

"Are you sure?" Cassie frowned.

"Go." Mirabel tipped her head toward the door.

Cassie pulled off her apron and hung it up. Then she grabbed her purse and hurried to the door. As she drove home, she hoped that she would be able to catch up with Tessa. She parked, then raced next door to Tessa's house. She knocked on the front door. After receiving no response, not even a bark from Harry, she walked around through the backyard. Two goats sauntered up to greet her.

"Hi boys, I can't play now." Cassie gave them each a pat then spotted Tessa already crossing Sebastian's property. "Tessa wait!" She shooed the goats away from the gate as she swung it closed.

Tessa turned to face her, while Harry plodded ahead a short distance.

"Cassie, I didn't know you were home."

"I just got home." Cassie reached her side, a bit out of breath, then smiled. "Can I go with you?"

"It's not always easy to get through the trails." Tessa looked over at her, then shrugged. "But if you want to, you're welcome to."

"I do." Cassie fell into step beside her. "I've been wanting to explore this area for a while. I didn't realize there was a trail on Sebastian's property until Oliver mentioned something about it."

"Yes, there are trails to the woods and cliffs on several private properties. Most of them are off limits, but Sebastian never minds if someone uses his trail." Tessa moved ahead of her as the trail became narrower.

"Is this the way that Clyde took then?" Cassie brushed a branch away from her face as she followed after her.

"Not likely, no. This is the longer way to go, but I don't want to step on anyone's toes. For Clyde to get to where he wanted to be, he would have been better off taking the trail on the dairy farm." Tessa glanced back at her. "But it's risky, the owner of the dairy farm doesn't like people trespassing on his property.

Not that I can blame him. Some people have no sense and they trample things, destroy plants, leave trash behind. It can get pretty bad. I think because he's a new owner, people don't pay much attention to his signs. The old owner never hassled anyone that wanted to use the trail."

"So, there's no access to the cliffs that isn't on private property?" Cassie shook her head. "That seems impossible."

"Actually, there are several trails that lead through the woods to the cliffs, but most hikers like to start their journey before dawn. There's nothing like seeing the sunrise over the mountain. And the park doesn't open its gates until after sunrise. So, it's not the most ideal way for everyone." Tessa pointed out a few broken branches ahead of them. "It looks like someone came through here recently." She grabbed one of the thin branches and sniffed the spot where it snapped. "Fresh, probably in the past day or two."

"But it could be anyone, right?" Cassie eyed the branch, then watched as she continued to walk along the trail. Again, she noticed Tessa's limp. She'd never thought too much about it, it was just part of who she was, but now she wondered.

"Sure, could be." Tessa cleared her throat, then whistled for Harry to come back to her side.

"Tessa, can I ask you something, a little personal?" Cassie maintained a close distance behind her.

"Sure, I guess. It doesn't mean I'll answer it, though."

"What happened to your leg?" Cassie held her breath as she wondered if she would be offended that she asked.

"That's a souvenir." Tessa gave her leg a light slap. "The only bullet I ever took. I was working a case that went sideways, and I got shot in the leg. On television they make it look like a bullet in the leg is no big deal, but it hit me in just the right place, I nearly bled out." She shook her head. "But I survived. Now, it's a reminder."

"A reminder of what?" Cassie gazed at her leg. Sometimes she forgot that Tessa was a retired police officer, who had likely lived quite an adventurous life before she met her.

"Of how short life can be." Tessa met her eyes. "That tomorrow is never promised. It doesn't make me all weepy or anything, but it keeps things in perspective. I'm sure you've experienced that, too."

"Me?" Cassie frowned as she continued down the trail. "No, I've never been shot."

"No, but you lost someone unexpectedly." Tessa glanced back at her. "When you lose someone before their time, it can wake you up to the reality of life, too, and just how few moments we might be given."

"True." Cassie took a deep breath as sharp emotions rocketed through her. "I've decided not to hold back, not to miss out."

"Admirable." Tessa nodded, then put her finger to her lips.

Cassie froze as she noticed the shift in Tessa's expression, from contemplative to stern.

CHAPTER 6

Tessa stared off through a patch of thick trees not far from them and didn't move a muscle.

Harry stuck his nose to the ground and huffed into the dirt. Then he dug one paw through it. He looked up at the same trees and started to march forward.

"Stay!" Tessa hissed at him as she crept forward as well.

Cassie started to follow Tessa, until she held up a hand to stop her.

Cassie froze, and took a breath. Whatever Tessa and Harry sensed beyond the trees, she couldn't detect. All she saw were leaves and branches. Her attention snapped slightly to the left as she heard a subtle crunch. Her stomach flipped as it was followed by another.

Footsteps? Could it be Aiden?

Had he been hiding from the police all of this time because he was somehow involved in Clyde's death? Had he gotten lost and was trying to find his way back home?

Cassie watched as Tessa edged her way forward. It wasn't hard to see her experience as a police officer, it was evident in her careful and crisp movements. She reached the patch of trees with Harry at her side. With one hand she slipped her phone out of her pocket, with her other, she pulled back a few branches to clear her view.

From behind Tessa, Cassie could see the screen of her phone, and realized that she was taking pictures of two young men.

Cassie's heart skipped a beat. The two men Oliver had mentioned? Criminals on the run? Had they stumbled onto their camp?

Tessa stepped back away from the trees and closer to Cassie. She thumbed through the pictures, still silent, then opened up her texts. She typed a few words, attached the pictures, then sent them off to Oliver.

A rustling beyond the trees made Cassie jump.

She felt the urge to hide, or at the very least to run. But she knew that any movement might draw the attention of the two men, who were likely armed.

Tessa put her hand on her shoulder and guided her back toward the path.

Cassie made every movement carefully, but still with every twig that snapped she braced herself for a volley of gunfire. Maybe she shouldn't have insisted on joining Tessa on her excursion. She guessed that they would hunker down behind the thick brush and wait for Oliver's arrival. Instead, as soon as she was tucked safely away, Tessa stepped forward again, with Harry right by her side.

"Tessa!" Cassie whispered, which drew a sharp glare from her.

As Cassie held her breath, Tessa moved toward the thick patch of trees.

Cassie knew that she wanted her to stay where she was. She guessed that she had been in far more dangerous situations than this, as a police officer. She moved with confidence, not a trace of hesitation.

But Cassie didn't see a police officer in front of her. She saw an older woman, with a limp. She saw her neighbor, someone who had been kind to her since she moved to Little Leaf Creek, someone she couldn't allow to walk into a dangerous situation alone. She imagined that Tessa would just watch them, but Cassie wanted to be prepared, just in case.

As Tessa stepped through the trees, Cassie began to move after her. But what could she do to help? She'd never been in a fight in her life, let alone stared down a gun. She glanced around for something to use as a weapon. Her eyes landed on a gnarled branch. It was almost too heavy for her to pick up, but she guessed that she could wield it if she had to. With her heart in her throat she followed after Tessa, and caught sight of the two men, just as a small branch fell from a tree beside Tessa. It made the men look up and straight at where Tessa was standing. Cassie's heart raced. Should they run? But before she could decide what to do, Tessa stepped toward them. The men jumped to their feet, obviously startled by her presence.

"Get down on the ground!" Tessa shouted as she glared at them both.

They stumbled back, but it only took both of them seconds to realize that Tessa was unarmed.

Harry leaned low to the ground and growled loudly.

Cassie tightened her grip on the branch even as her arms ached from holding it.

"Look at this old woman." The young man with long, black hair and a scraggly blue t-shirt laughed. "What are you going to do, make a citizen's arrest?"

"You going to stick that puppy on us?" The taller of the pair with sandy blond hair and a deep voice, chuckled. "You'd better get back to your walk, you old fool, before we decide to get rid of you."

Cassie's heart raced as she realized that she had walked into the middle of a fight that they likely could not win.

"I said get on the ground now, this is your last warning!" Tessa shouted.

"Who's that you got with you?" The first man peered past Tessa at Cassie. "What's that you got, honey? What do you think a bit of wood is going to do?" He broke into loud laughter.

Tessa glanced back over her shoulder. Her eyes glowed with anger as they briefly met Cassie's. As she turned back, the taller man reached for the gun on the ground beside him.

"Now, Harry!" Tessa barked.

Harry snarled as he plowed into the man who reached for the gun.

"Ow!" The man yelled as he landed on the ground in the same moment that his partner, who

PERIL IN LITTLE LEAF CREEK

was distracted by Harry, was tackled by Tessa and pinned to the ground.

"Get off of me!" The man shrieked at Tessa.

"Let go! Let go! Somebody stop this beast!" The man under Harry tried to squirm out from under him.

"Down on the ground! Get down on the ground!" Oliver's voice boomed from just behind Cassie.

Cassie saw the barrel of his gun first, as he moved past her with his arms outstretched and the weapon aimed at the man that Harry still restrained.

Tessa managed to get the man on the ground turned onto his stomach, and pinned his arms behind him, while Oliver kicked the gun away from the man that Harry had detained. Cassie was shocked by Tessa's strength.

"Release, Harry!" Oliver commanded the dog with the same familiarity that Cassie had heard Tessa use. Harry ran over to Oliver's side. Oliver tossed a pair of handcuffs to Tessa then rubbed Harry's ear. "Good boy."

Tessa caught the handcuffs right out of midair, and snapped them onto the wrists of the man she had subdued.

Oliver requested a medic on his radio, then

holstered his weapon. He looked over at Cassie, his eyes narrowed.

"Cassie, put that down."

Only then did she realize that she still held the branch in her hands. She let it crash to the ground as her muscles ached from holding it up for so long.

Oliver stared at her for a moment longer, then looked over at Tessa.

"You want to explain all this to me?"

"You got here fast." Tessa dusted off her hands as she walked over to Oliver.

"I was at the crime scene nearby when I got your text." Oliver crossed his arms as he studied Tessa. "I'm guessing that is where you were headed when you came across these two."

"Might have been." Tessa shrugged.

"You should have waited for me to get here before you confronted them." Oliver shook his head. "They were armed!"

"They heard us and we had to do something. They didn't cause us too much trouble, did they, Harry?" Tessa smiled as the dog ran to her side. "Besides, I had my back-up." She grinned at Cassie.

"Exactly." Cassie rubbed her arm as she wondered if Tessa's words were a compliment or a tease.

"I can't believe you involved her in this." Oliver's tone hardened.

"I believe I involved myself in it." Cassie felt a touch of annoyance as Oliver looked over at her again. "Aren't you glad they've been captured?"

"Yes." Oliver cleared his throat. "I'm sorry, Cassie, but you should have waited for me before you went anywhere near them. It was too big a risk. It could have gone badly."

"But it didn't." Cassie looked into his eyes. "Everyone's fine."

"Not me!" The taller man on the ground bellowed. "I'm not fine! He tackled me!"

"Relax, Harry just made sure you didn't do something you would regret." Oliver tossed his words in the direction of the man, but turned his focus on Tessa. "You never should have brought Cassie out here. You never should have come out here." He turned his attention back to Cassie. "I warned you that there were fugitives in these woods, a man has died, and you still thought it would be a good idea to come here?"

"She was with me." Tessa stepped up beside Cassie. "She doesn't need to be sheltered. She's strong, and determined."

"Go. I'll get your statements later." Oliver looked at Tessa. "And stay away from my crime scene."

"Let's go, Tessa." Cassie started toward the trail. "Oliver has work to do."

"Yes, he does." Tessa's gaze remained on Oliver for a few moments longer, then she followed Cassie onto the trail.

CHAPTER 7

As Cassie and Tessa made their way back toward the clearing on Sebastian's property, Cassie tried to sort through the entire experience. Seeing Tessa in action had taken her by surprise. Although she had no doubt about how sharp her mind was, it impressed her that she was able to handle the criminals physically as well.

Tessa rested her fingertips on the back gate of her fence and turned to look at Cassie.

"Why don't you come in? We can try to figure all of this out."

"I'd like that." Cassie nodded as she followed after her.

Harry barked a friendly hello at the goats who barely looked up at him.

Cassie gave them each a pat as she walked by. She had definitely become more used to them over the last few weeks.

Cassie's thoughts traveled back to Oliver on the mountain. She found him too harsh at times, yet something about him still drew her in. Was it his desire to protect her? His determination to get to the truth? An uneasy thought crept into her mind. Was she attracted to him? There was no doubt that he was a handsome man, but after her husband's death she'd settled into the idea that the time for romance in her life had come to an end. She brushed off the thoughts and focused on following Tessa through her back door and into her kitchen.

Tessa walked right up to a cupboard and opened it.

"What are you doing?" Cassie watched as she began pulling mixing bowls out of it.

"This calls for cheesecake." Tessa raised her eyebrows as she walked over to a few boxes of cream cheese, eggs and sour cream that were on the counter. "It won't take long to get ready, but it won't be ready for a few hours, just talk me through what we know so far." She set a box of graham crackers, a plastic bag and a rolling pin down on the counter in front of Cassie. "You can work on crushing the crackers for the crust."

"Okay." Cassie smiled as she opened the box. "Did you do this when you were working as a police officer?"

"I didn't have time then. Growing up I loved to bake with my mother and Alice, my friend." Tessa pulled out her mixer. "But when I joined the force, I spent most of my time at my desk digging through paperwork. But—" She paused.

"But what?" Cassie opened a package of crackers as she looked up at her.

"Those late nights, they were difficult for me. I would often forget to eat, or just not have an appetite even if food was offered to me." Tessa cleared her throat.

"It's hard to concentrate with no food in your belly." Cassie frowned as she crushed the crackers.

"Yeah, it could be. I would get shaky, sometimes even get migraines, because I wouldn't keep track of how long I'd gone without eating." Tessa shook her head. "Alice noticed this. Whenever I was working long hours she'd show up at the station with food. At first it was a sandwich, but then she noticed I would often not eat it. So, she started making me things I couldn't resist." She smiled some as she began to mix together the cream cheese and sugar. "She made me the most delicious cakes, cookies and pies."

"Aw, how sweet!" Cassie grinned as she imagined a younger Tessa feasting on the delicacies while she pored over paperwork.

"It was." Tessa cleared her throat. "Back to the case. What do we know so far?" She cracked an egg.

"What happened to her? Your friend?" Cassie locked her eyes to Tessa's profile as she leaned over the bowl.

"We know that Clyde died, and we know that it wasn't an accident." Tessa pursed her lips as she turned on the mixer.

Cassie received the clear message that she would not talk about Alice any further. At least not at the moment. When she turned off the mixer, Cassie spoke up.

"We know that it looked like he died accidentally. So, it's possible that the killer went to some trouble to make it look that way."

"Right."

"And that Clyde was alone in his tent when he was found, even though he was supposed to be camping with a young man, Aiden, who is currently missing." Cassie shook the bag of crackers a bit, then began to crush them again. "Which makes Aiden a prime suspect, don't you think?" She winced at the thought, knowing that Mirabel considered him family.

"Maybe, but we also know there were two criminals camping in the woods not far from his camp. Maybe they happened upon him, and afraid that he would turn them in, they killed him?" Tessa shook her head. "Maybe they would have shot him. But I can't see them staging a death like that. It's possible, though." She turned to look at her. "Also, we do know that Clyde had another enemy who was in town."

"Who?" Cassie narrowed her eyes, then took a sharp breath. "Do you mean Trevor's father?"

"Yes, I do." Tessa shrugged. "Maybe he wanted to get rid of his competition for his son's affection."

"I'm not so sure that he's interested in his son's affection." Cassie placed the crushed crackers in a bowl, added the sugar and melted butter that Tessa had given her and stirred. "But it is strange that he happened to be in town when this happened."

"Without actually getting to see the crime scene, we can only assume what might have happened." Tessa turned on the mixer again. "I doubt that the police have left anything there, though."

As Cassie listened to the whir of the machine her

thoughts journeyed back to the moment that Trevor burst through the door, announcing that the death had not been an accident.

"Maybe we should find out what Trevor knows. From what I understand he was close to Clyde, he's probably our best resource for finding out more about him." Cassie dug her phone out of her purse. "I can give him a call and arrange to meet with him. Or maybe I'll just go see if he's in the alley first."

"That's a good place to start." Tessa nodded at her as she worked on the crust. "Good job. That's going to be great."

"I hope so." Cassie smiled as she thought of Tessa's friend preparing her sweet treats to make sure that she ate. "I think we should look into Clyde's business contacts, too. If anything was going on in his professional life, they might have more information. I think Sebastian mentioned something about him going into business with someone. I'll have to double-check with him, I don't remember the name."

"Shane?" Tessa turned back to the oven. "Shane Carlo?"

"I think it was Shane." Cassie nodded. "I'm not sure about the last name, though."

"I can get in touch with Shane." Tessa slid the

springform pan into the oven just as someone knocked on the front door.

"Cassie, are you in there?"

Cassie looked up at the sound of Sebastian's voice. Immediately, her heart skipped a beat. She couldn't deny that she liked his company. But was it more than that?

"What does he want?" Tessa frowned as she walked to the door. She opened it, but blocked Sebastian's entrance. "Can I help you?"

"Tessa, I just wanted to see if Cassie was here. I went to her place, but no one answered."

"I'm here, Sebastian." Cassie walked up behind Tessa.

"Oh good." Sebastian breathed a sigh of relief, then shook his head. "After I heard about what happened in the woods, I was worried that you might have been involved."

"Why would you think that?" Cassie glanced over at Tessa.

"I heard it was Harry that helped catch the criminals, and I know how much time you two spend together." Sebastian glanced at Tessa, then looked back at Cassie. "Tessa took you up there, didn't she?"

"I asked to go with her." Cassie crossed her arms. "And I'm glad I did."

"It's dangerous, Cassie, you could have been hurt." Sebastian frowned as he walked past Tessa and into the house.

"But I wasn't." Cassie shrugged and looked over at Tessa. "Tessa took down two fugitives with a little help from Harry. She was amazing."

"Alright, that's enough." Tessa rolled her eyes.

"Still, you shouldn't have been there in the first place." Sebastian pulled off his baseball cap and ran his hand through his hair. "I know that everyone's calling Clyde's death an accident, but I don't think it was."

"No one thinks it was." Tessa frowned.

"Do you know anything about Clyde?" Cassie met Sebastian's eyes. "Anything that might explain how this happened to him?"

"We went to high school together. He was younger than me." Sebastian shook his head. "We weren't exactly friends, he ran in different circles to me. If he wasn't alone he was always with the jocks."

"You weren't a jock?" Cassie glanced over his fit frame.

"Not even close." Sebastian laughed. "I was more

into drama and band. But we did cross paths a time or two. He seemed like a good guy."

"What about his personal life?" Cassie frowned. "Was he dating anyone? Married?"

"Not that I know of, but I think you'd have to talk to his closer friends to find out more about that." Sebastian sniffed the air. "What is that delicious smell?"

"Cheesecake. Want to come in and have some?" Cassie stepped to the side.

"Wait a minute." Tessa held up one hand. "It will be a while until it's ready. It still has to be refrigerated for a few hours. I'm sure that Sebastian has other things to do."

"Uh, right." Sebastian forced a smile. "Maybe another time." He met Cassie's eyes. "If you feel up to it we can do some more work on the house later."

"Thank you. I'll let you know." Cassie nodded as Tessa shut the door. "Tessa, you don't have to be so rude to him." She frowned.

"You shouldn't invite people into my home." Tessa shook her head. "I'm pretty selective about my guests."

"You have a problem with Sebastian?" Cassie followed her back into the kitchen.

"Not with Sebastian exactly. He's actually a nice

young man. I have a problem with the way he hangs around you." Tessa plopped down in one of the kitchen chairs.

"Excuse me?" Cassie narrowed her eyes.

"The man's lovesick over you, you can't tell? I don't know who is worse, him or Oliver." Tessa rolled her eyes.

"That's just ridiculous." Cassie sat down across from her. "Neither of them is interested in me. You're seeing things that aren't there."

"You can't be that blind, can you?" Tessa stared at her. "He's practically rebuilding your house for you."

"I didn't ask him to." Cassie crossed her arms. "He refuses to let me pay him."

"Exactly!"

"Ugh, Tessa. You're crazy." Cassie laughed. "I'm going to go find Trevor and see if he can tell me anything more about Clyde."

"Alright, I'll get in touch with Shane." Tessa watched as Cassie walked toward the door. "You can deny it all you want, Cassie, but eventually those two are going to come to blows over you."

Cassie pulled the door shut behind her without responding. How could she? She didn't want to believe that Tessa was right, but she couldn't deny that she'd sensed some tension between Sebastian and Oliver when they were together. Could it really be about her? The thought sent her mind spinning. She couldn't imagine what either of them saw in her.

Cassie pushed the thoughts away as she headed for the alley in town where she knew that Trevor liked to work. By the time she reached the alley, her thoughts had drifted back to the two men in custody. Had Oliver been able to get a confession out of them? Had they been the ones to murder Clyde?

"Trevor?" Cassie peeked down the alley which was cluttered with an assortment of scrap metal. Although she couldn't see him, she could hear his voice.

"You don't have any business being here!"

Cassie took a step back as his voice echoed down the alley. "Trevor, I just want to talk!" She called out.

"Don't even try that with me!" Trevor's angry voice reached her again. "I don't want your money! I don't want anything from you!"

It dawned on her that Trevor wasn't speaking to her, he was speaking to someone else. Her heart skipped a beat as she wondered who had him that angry.

"Don't you walk away from me, boy!" A thicker,

older voice carried down the alley, followed by the sounds of a scuffle.

"Trevor!" Cassie gasped as she hurried down the alley. She wanted to be as brave as she'd seen Tessa be, but the truth was, she tried to shy away from anger, and she could hear plenty of it in the shouts that the two men began to exchange. She stepped around a large, metal sheet that leaned against one side of the alley and took in the sight of Trevor, and another man, who loomed over him.

CHAPTER 8

"Dad stop! You haven't visited for years! We thought you were dead." Trevor shouted at him, his voice so filled with frustration that it cracked from the weight of it. "No one wants you here!"

"I didn't ask to be invited." The older man took a step back, then settled his gaze on Cassie. "Why don't you just move along? There's nothing to see here."

"I'm not going anywhere!" Cassie narrowed her eyes as she stared straight at him. "You need to back off before I call the police to make you back off."

"Oh, you're going to call the police because I'm having a conversation with my son?" His voice raised as he took a step toward her.

"Dad, no." Trevor moved between them. "Cassie is a friend of mine."

"A friend? She's a little too old to be a friend, don't you think?" He scowled at Cassie.

"I'm a fan of his art." Cassie glanced between the two and wondered if she had stepped into something that she shouldn't have. "Trevor, are you okay?"

"I'm fine, Cassie, it's okay." Trevor lowered his eyes.

"That's right, he's fine, so you need to be on your way." He shook his head as he continued to glare at her. "People in small towns have to be so nosy."

"I'm not going anywhere until I'm sure that Trevor is okay. It didn't sound like he was okay when I heard you two shouting from the other end of the alley." Cassie crossed her arms.

"Look, we just had a misunderstanding. Right Trev?" He turned his attention to his son.

"It's not a misunderstanding, Dad. I told you I want nothing to do with you, nothing has changed. You had your chance to be a father when I was a kid. I haven't seen you in over ten years. Now, you don't even exist to me, so please, stay out of my way." Trevor turned and began to walk back down the alley.

"I'm not saying I haven't made mistakes, Trevor." His shoulders drooped as he watched his son walk away. His eyes shifted to Cassie's. "Haven't you ever made a mistake?"

Cassie's heart pounded as her mind flashed back to the final years she'd spent with her husband. She couldn't count the number of mistakes she felt she'd made. They stayed together because it was convenient, because they were scared of change, but in reality they no longer loved each other.

"It's probably best if you give him a little time. He's dealing with quite a loss right now." Cassie took a deep breath and focused. "His friend Clyde Timpson died. Did you know him?"

"Clyde?" He narrowed his eyes. "Yes, I knew him. He died?"

"Yes, and Trevor is taking it pretty hard." Cassie glanced down the alley at the young man who had begun to sort through a pile of metal pipes. "He really admired the man."

"I bet." He pursed his lips.

"We haven't properly met." She held out her hand to him. "I'm Cassie."

"Ron." He gave her hand a quick shake then pulled his away. "I'm sure you think I'm a terrible person."

"I don't think that." Cassie tried to keep her expression neutral.

"Don't feel badly about it, everyone in this town thinks it. I took off, and left behind a pregnant cheerleader. But we've all done stupid things, huh?" Ron shrugged. "Mine was just a big, stupid thing."

"It's easy to make the wrong choice and harder to live with it." Cassie nodded. "I suppose Clyde didn't go easy on you either."

"No, he didn't." Ron balled his hands into fists. "He was always so smug. The last time we talked, over ten years ago, I just wanted to wipe that smirk off his face. But I didn't. I walked away." He sighed. "I guess it was better than throwing a punch, but sometimes I wonder if I had made a different decision, maybe my son would see me differently."

"Trevor's still young. Give him time." Cassie cleared her throat. "I'm sure it's quite a surprise for him to even find out that you're in town. Did anyone know you were coming?"

"No, I just decided to stop in. I had hoped to make some progress with him and make up for lost time, but it doesn't look like that's going to happen." Ron shook his head.

"When did you get into town?" Cassie attempted

to sound casual, but heard the hint of tension in her own voice. Would he notice?

"Yesterday." Ron ran the back of his hand across his forehead. "I wanted to talk to Trevor right away, but I just couldn't work up the nerve."

"So, what did you do? Just hang out? Meet up with some old friends?" Cassie held back the question she wanted to ask. Did you go for a hike and kill your rival for your son's affections? That might make it pretty clear that she suspected him of murder.

"I just drove around. Relived some memories." Ron settled his gaze on hers. "What's with all the questions?"

"I'm just curious." Cassie bit into her bottom lip as she realized she might have gone a bit too far.

"Curious huh?" Ron spread his shoulders wider as he turned to fully face her. "In my experience, anyone who asks a lot of questions is up to something."

"I'm not." Cassie felt her chest tighten as he focused in on her.

"I think you might be." Ron scowled at her, then glanced away, down the alley at Trevor. "It doesn't matter, though. Whatever you're up to, it's not going to make any difference. One day that kid is going to realize that he wants a relationship with me, that I'm the best thing he's got, and then it won't matter what you say about me, what his mother says about me, or what anyone in this tiny little town says." He turned and walked off down the other side of the alley.

Cassie stared after him, uncertain how to read his passion. Was he that determined to create a relationship with his son, or was he trying to use him as an alibi, a reason that he was in town? As much as she wanted to know what Ron's involvement with the murder was, she didn't think she would get much more out of him.

Cassie looked over at Trevor and noticed his downward turned eyes and drooped shoulders

"Are you okay?"

"You've met him now. Great guy, isn't he?" Trevor glanced up at her briefly, then looked back down at the sheet of metal that reflected his tense expression.

"I know there's a lot going on between the two of you, Trevor. I'm sorry that he is giving you such a hard time." Cassie frowned as she studied his reflection. She could see pain etched through his tightened lips and furrowed brow.

"Now you're going to say that all parents try their hardest, right?" Trevor looked up at her.

"I wouldn't know. I've never had children." Cassie smiled slightly. "You are an amazing young man, and a very talented artist. I do know that my parents tried their hardest for me and that your father may not be the parent you'd like him to be, but that shouldn't stop you from being who you are and who you want to be."

"Thanks Cassie." Trevor smiled and looked into her eyes. "That actually does help."

"Good." Cassie didn't want to think about how Trevor might react if it turned out that his father was involved in Clyde's murder. How would he handle it if he was?

CHAPTER 9

The shrill shriek of sirens in the distance drew Cassie's attention to the end of the alley. She and Trevor began to walk toward the sound, just as Sebastian crossed in front of the alley.

"Sebastian!" Cassie waved at him as she quickened her pace with Trevor close behind.

"Cassie." Sebastian paused, then nodded to Trevor. "Trevor."

"What's with all of the lights and sirens?" Cassie stopped at the end of the alley, with Trevor at her side.

"Some kind of development in the investigation." Sebastian shrugged. "Not sure exactly what yet. But I've heard rumors that a witness they were looking for came forward."

"A witness?" Cassie shook her head. "Who would that be? The only other person there with him was Aiden." She gasped. "Oh, did they find Aiden?"

"Maybe. I don't know who it is." Sebastian frowned.

A mixture of joy and trepidation flowed through Cassie. What did this mean for Mirabel? She was glad that Aiden had been found, hopefully safe, but would the police discover that he'd had something to do with Clyde's murder?

"It's not going to help anything." Trevor scoffed as he kicked the sole of his shoe against the pavement.

"What do you mean?" Cassie looked over at him. "If he was there around the time of Clyde's death he can at least give some insight into what might have happened."

"But he wasn't there. He couldn't have been." Trevor sighed. "That's what I kept trying to tell Ollie. If Aiden was there he never would have left Clyde alone. Even if he was afraid for his own life, he wouldn't have left him alone."

"But you can't know that for sure. Aiden was supposed to be climbing and camping with him." Cassie frowned. "Sometimes you think you know what someone is like, but it turns out that you didn't know them that well after all."

"I know Aiden. I've known him his whole life." Trevor shook his head. "Sorry Cassie, but you have no idea what you're talking about. Aiden is a good guy, he's like a superhero. He would do anything to help anyone. If he was there with Clyde, he would have done whatever it took to save him."

"I agree." Sebastian smiled at Cassie. "He's a good kid."

"This is just like Oliver to waste his time hunting down the wrong guy." Trevor looked from Sebastian to Cassie.

"Oliver is doing his best, Trevor." Cassie looked over at him. "He's a good detective, and I'm sure he's going to figure out what happened. Aiden is just a first step in what might be a long process."

"I don't see why it has to be so long." Trevor sighed. "Whoever was in the woods with Clyde is the one who killed him."

"One step at a time, Trevor. Cassie is right. Oliver is good at his job, and he's going to get to the truth." Sebastian met Cassie's eyes briefly, then looked away. "I should get going, I have to get a few things from the hardware store. Let me know what you find out when you speak to Oliver." He gave her a short wave then continued down the street.

As Cassie stared after Sebastian, she wondered why he assumed she would speak to Oliver, and whether she had imagined the tension in his voice when he spoke about him. He was right about his assumption. She did intend to talk to Oliver. She wanted to find out what had developed in the case, and she wanted to be sure that she wasn't making Trevor false promises. She also wanted to mention her conversation with Ron.

"I'll see what I can find out." Cassie smiled at Trevor. "You should get to work. Emotional times bring out the best in artists, right?"

"So they say. I guess I can give it a try." Trevor turned to start walking back down the alley.

Cassie continued down the street in the direction of the police station. Part of her was tempted to call Tessa and give her an update, but she didn't really have anything to tell her. Not yet at least.

As Cassie stepped into the station, she noticed a flurry of activity all around her. Officers in patrol uniforms were scattered in all directions. A large gathering of locals filled up the area right in front of the reception desk. The officers manning the desk appeared overwhelmed as various people shouted questions at them. She noticed a few journalists huddled together near the entrance of the interior of the station, devices in hand, ready to record whatever might happen next. She presumed that some of them must have come from outside Little Leaf Creek. She couldn't imagine that their small town had so many journalists.

Cassie stepped up beside a woman she recognized, Sharon from the salon.

"What's going on here?" Cassie whispered the question, eager not to draw too much attention to herself.

"The journalists are here to find out more about Clyde's death. I think a rumor is going around that it wasn't an accident. Some of the locals are here because they found that young man that was supposed to be on the mountain with Clyde. Aiden." Sharon looked over at Cassie. "They took him in. His mother is so upset, they had no reason to take him in, they could have just questioned him at home. I love Ollie, you know, but he didn't need to bring Aiden down to the station." She crossed her arms. "The locals are here to try and get him released."

Cassie followed Sharon's gaze which had settled on a large man with thick, red hair walking in their direction.

"Devin." Sharon called out to him. He looked over, his eyes widened with recognition as he walked toward her.

"Hi Sharon." Devin nodded.

"What are you doing here?" Sharon smiled.

"The police wanted to ask me a few questions about Clyde." Devin put his hands in his pockets and rocked back on his heels.

"Oh, are you a suspect?" Sharon frowned.

"A suspect?" Devin laughed. "No, it was an accident. They wanted some information on the—" he lowered his voice and stepped closer to her. "The stove."

"Really? Do they really think it was an accident?" Sharon asked.

"That's what they said. But there's a rumor going around that it was murder." Devin looked from Sharon to Cassie.

"Sorry, I'm so rude." Sharon gestured to Cassie. "Devin, this is Cassie. Cassie's new in town. She works at Mirabel's. Devin owns a camping store and adventure place, Adventures Aplenty, in Calhoon."

"Nice to meet you." Devin smiled widely, as he offered his hand.

"You, too." Cassie shook his hand and smiled in return.

"I better get going, I have to open the shop." Devin walked away.

Cassie turned back just as Oliver stepped through the door and into the gathering of journalists.

As they shouted questions at him, he met her eyes through the crowd.

Cassie felt the instinct to look away, but something about the way he clung to the visual connection made her keep her gaze steadily locked with his.

"I know everyone has questions about what happened to Clyde, but for the moment I cannot comment on an ongoing investigation. You must allow us to do our work."

"Free Aiden!" Someone in the crowd close to Cassie shouted. Sharon joined in.

"Free Aiden! Free Aiden!" She chanted, along with the crowd.

Cassie continued to stare into Oliver's eyes as she sensed the tension mount within him. He turned back toward the door, and stepped through it. She noticed that he didn't close it behind him. Despite this, the journalists didn't follow him. She guessed that they knew the rules of engagement when it came to questioning the police. However, she didn't know of any rule that said she couldn't follow Oliver. Maybe he wanted her to. Maybe that was why he had left the door open. Her heart raced as she considered whether to follow after him. What was the worst that he would do? She doubted he would arrest her, maybe he'd insist that she leave, but that was worth the risk.

CHAPTER 10

Cassie waited until the attention of the reporters had turned to Aiden's supporters, then she made her way through the still open door in the police station that led down a short hallway into a wide open space filled with desks. She knew from being a suspect in a murder investigation when she had first arrived in Little Leaf Creek, which office was Oliver's.

Cassie walked over to it. As she approached the open door, Oliver dropped down into a chair behind his desk. He looked up as she peered around the doorway.

Cassie braced herself for a lecture.

"Hey Cassie." Oliver gestured to a chair on the other side of his desk. "Have a seat."

"Sorry to bother you, Oliver, I just wanted to talk to you about something." Cassie eased down into the chair, still uncertain about whether he really wanted her there.

"If it's about bringing Aiden in for questioning, you have to understand, Aiden hasn't been cooperative. He won't answer our questions. He tried to run away from the officers. Despite the rumors, we haven't arrested him, we are just questioning him."

"No, it's not about Aiden." Cassie smiled. "It's about Trevor's father, Ron."

"What about Ron?" Oliver scooted his chair closer to the desk and met her eyes. "I haven't been able to track him down yet."

"I just spoke to him. He was with Trevor." Cassie cleared her throat.

"Trevor? I asked him to call me the moment that he had any contact with his father." Oliver narrowed his eyes. "Not that I really expected him to listen. Why didn't you call me?"

"I wasn't sure if you had spoken to him already, and besides, he left before I had the chance to. I knew that you had been looking for him, and I thought I should mention seeing him to you." Cassie shifted in her chair. "I'm sorry, I probably should have called you."

"It's alright. I probably wouldn't have answered as I was in the middle of things with Aiden. I guess Ron was spending time with his son then?" Oliver continued to hold her gaze.

"I'm not sure if that's exactly how I would describe it. It was more like they were arguing." Cassie glanced down at his cluttered desk. She hadn't expected it to be cluttered. She was sure it was neat and tidy the last time she saw it, but maybe she hadn't noticed the mess because he had been questioning her on suspicion of murder at the time. Oliver seemed like such an organized person.

"They were arguing?" Oliver rested his elbows on his desk and leaned closer to her. "About Clyde?"

"No, it wasn't about Clyde. But I did ask Ron about Clyde, and he definitely has an issue with him. I also found out that he got into town yesterday, and claims that he was just driving around, so my guess is that he doesn't have any alibi for the time of Clyde's murder." Cassie bit into her bottom lip as she wondered if she'd already said too much.

"Death. The time of his death." Oliver frowned. "It hasn't been ruled a homicide."

"You know that he wouldn't have made a mistake

like that, Oliver." Cassie narrowed her eyes as she studied him. "I know that you do."

"Now, you're suddenly an expert on Clyde?" Oliver raised his eyebrows. "I thought you were new to town?"

"Yes, you're right, I'm not an expert on Clyde. But I don't believe an experienced camper would make a mistake like that. I believe what Trevor told me. Tessa and Sebastian don't believe it could be an accident. They don't believe that Clyde would have ever put that stove in his tent." Cassie sat back in her chair and crossed her arms. "Is it really so far-fetched to think that it could have been a murder?"

"Well, if Sebastian says so." Oliver shrugged, then cleared his throat. "I'm sorry, it's been a rough day so far. Look, I'm not ruling out that it was a homicide, but I have to go where the evidence leads. Right now there is no sign of foul play. He died from carbon monoxide poisoning. But without some kind of indication that he was murdered, it very well could have been an accident. His time of death is estimated to be between about seven and nine that night. Maybe he was cold so he put the stove in his tent. Maybe he was just lazy. It looks like he fell and hit the back of his head. Maybe he had a little too much to drink and passed out and hit his head before he turned the stove off. Maybe he tripped, hit his head and that caused him to lose consciousness, that would explain what happened. There are several explanations, all of which would be easy enough to believe, if there was a second person there to see what happened." He ran his fingers back through his hair. "Hopefully, Aiden will speak to me. He is being looked over by the medics."

"Trevor doesn't think that he was in the woods with Clyde. He says that Aiden never would have left Clyde behind if something happened to him." Cassie tilted her head to the side as she watched tension ripple through his expression. "Do you know Aiden well?"

"I know him well enough." One of Oliver's hands curled into a fist on his desk. "That's why I had hoped that he would turn himself in, instead we had to hunt him down. Yes, he has a good reputation. He's never been in any trouble before. He's always been involved in charitable programs, he's squeaky clean. There's not much about him that would indicate he would want to hide from us. Which makes the fact that he did hide from us, even more concerning. He also tried to run from the officer when he tried to speak to him. No matter what

Trevor says, Aiden knows something. Cassie, my instincts tell me that."

"Do you think he's just scared?" Cassie lowered her voice as she studied him. "Maybe he heard the police were looking for him, and he got scared."

"If he's scared, then he still has something to tell us." Oliver sighed as he shook his head.

"What about the two criminals that we found yesterday? Did they have anything to say about Clyde?" Cassie attempted to keep her tone casual.

"Neither has said a word. Both wanted a lawyer. I haven't been able to get anything out of them. If they ever saw Clyde, they're not admitting to it. They are suspects of course, because of their history, and they were in the vicinity." Oliver glanced at his phone as it buzzed. "They're done with Aiden. I have to go speak with him and see what I can find out." He looked back up at her. "Cassie, I know you're wrapped up in this, and I know that you and Tessa have become friends, but you need to understand that this is an active investigation, and getting into the middle of it can cause a lot of harm."

"You want me to stay out of it?" Cassie stood up from her chair, prepared to defend herself and her actions.

"I'm just asking you to be careful. Tessa likes to

go in guns blazing." Oliver stood up as well. "As of now, I have no proof that Clyde was murdered, but when I do come across that proof, I will find his murderer."

Oliver's words sank in as she nodded. She noticed the fact that Oliver didn't say if he found proof of a murder, he said when. As she held his gaze she realized that he believed just as much as the rest of them, that Clyde's death hadn't been an accident. He was just waiting for the proof that it was murder.

"I don't want to cause you any trouble, Oliver, I hope you know that." Cassie frowned as she looked down at her shoes. "It was my idea to go into the woods with Tessa, not hers. She's a good person."

"I know she is." Oliver sighed deeply. "But she's reckless. It's one thing when she takes these chances with her own life, there's nothing I can do about that. But it's another when she involves someone else." He stepped closer to her. "You."

"I understand your concern, but you don't need to worry about me." Cassie looked straight back at him and willed herself to feel the confidence she tried to convey. "I can take care of myself."

"I'm sure that you can." Oliver smiled. "But just be careful. I should really get to work on this."

"Okay, hopefully you get a break in the case

soon." Cassie walked with him back through the police station. "If there's anything you think I can do to help, just let me know."

Oliver met her eyes briefly and smiled slightly.

Cassie hurried out the door in the direction of the parking lot, she was even more determined to try and help find Clyde's killer.

With Aiden being taken in for questioning, she decided it would be a good idea to check in with Mirabel.

CHAPTER 11

As Cassie drove to the diner, she noticed several people gathered outside the doors, and the parking lot packed with cars.

Of course, the news of Aiden being found had obviously spread throughout town and the residents had gathered at the diner to discuss it. It looked like most of the crowd that had been at the police station was now at the diner.

Cassie stepped into the chaos of the overcrowded dining room and spotted Mirabel juggling two trays of food.

"Let me get that." Cassie took one of the trays from her. "It's wild in here! Why didn't you call?"

"Honestly, I haven't had the chance to breathe, let alone make a call." Mirabel rushed the tray of food in her hands over to a nearby table. "That goes to table five." She called over her shoulder.

Cassie snapped into action and served the food to the waiting diners. The rush didn't die down for another hour, and when it did, people left in small spurts instead of all at once. The conversations that carried back and forth across tables focused on Clyde's death, Aiden's involvement, and the two men that had been hiding out in the woods. Cassie also heard snippets of conversations about Ron's presence in town. None of it sounded new, or terribly accurate to her.

"Whew." Mirabel wiped her hand across her forehead as the last group of customers left the diner, leaving behind just a few stragglers that appeared to be more interested in their coffees and phones than gossip. "What a crazy afternoon." She shook her head as she leaned her elbows on the counter. "What I need after that kind of crazy, is a good milkshake. Want one?"

Cassie smiled at the thought.

"Actually, that sounds perfect. But I should make them, you've got to be exhausted."

"No worries, I'm fine." Mirabel turned around to the blender. "Besides, I make the best caramel milkshakes in town, you don't want to miss out on it."

"I certainly don't." Cassie watched as Mirabel moved smoothly between the freezer and the blender. "How are you really holding up with everything that happened to Aiden?"

"I spoke to his mother." Mirabel paused as she turned on the blender. When the loud whirring stopped, she looked over her shoulder at Cassie. "She said the police's version is true. Aiden was startled when the police announced their presence and he panicked and ran. They didn't arrest him, they just took him in for questioning. I still say they didn't need to take him to the police station for questioning, but she seems to feel differently. She says she's relieved that Aiden wasn't hurt because he ran from the police." She rolled her eyes. "Apparently, he also had a knife on him."

"Really?" Cassie's eyes widened as the blender turned back on. Once it cut off again she spoke up. "Why did Aiden have a knife on him?"

"According to June, he always has one on him when he is going camping. She had the chance to speak with him briefly. He told her that Clyde had changed his mind at the last minute and told Aiden that he couldn't come with him on the trip." Mirabel sighed. "I've never known this kid to lie."

"But he's probably scared." Cassie winced as she considered the possibility. "Maybe he's backed into a corner, and he's making up the best story he can."

"I'm not saying that it's not possible, but I don't believe it. I think he's telling the truth. The problem is, he says that Clyde called him. There's no way to prove what they said to each other. Aiden's alibi is that he parked on a cliff and threw some rocks off the side for the next few hours and then slept in his car. I don't think that's going to cut it with the police."

"No, I don't think so, either." Cassie settled on one of the barstools. "But if he wasn't there, then why did Clyde change his mind? Was he planning to meet someone else?"

"Aiden didn't have anything else to say. I told him not to talk to the cops unless he has a lawyer with him." Mirabel pursed her lips, then shook her head. "Not that he'll be able to afford one." Her voice trembled. "I'm sorry, Cassie, this is all just a bit much for me."

"I know it is." Cassie nodded. "I can understand why you're worried. We'll just have to make sure we figure out who is actually responsible for Clyde's death. Then Aiden will be out of the crossfire."

"And how are we going to figure that out?" Mirabel slumped forward, tiredness evident in the droop of her eyelids.

"We need to figure out who was after Clyde. Who would do this to him? Did he have any enemies? Who are his friends?" Cassie frowned. "Somewhere in his daily life, I bet there's a clue that will lead us to the right person. If only he had a girlfriend or a wife, we might be able to get more details on who the murderer might be."

"A wife or a girlfriend would never happen with Clyde. He was a self-proclaimed bachelor and proud of it. He'd laugh at anyone who even thought about getting married." Mirabel rolled her eyes. "He would say, no woman could tame his love for adventure."

"Great, a loner. If he never had anyone close to him, then we're not going to find out much about his personal life."

"He wasn't always alone." Mirabel took a long sip of her milkshake.

"Huh?" Cassie looked up at her. "I thought you said he was."

"I said he always said he was single, I didn't say he was always alone." Mirabel raised an eyebrow. "I think he wanted everyone to believe that he was single. But I saw him in here more than once with the same girl, and the way they spoke to each other, the way they interacted with each other, there's no way that they weren't together in some way."

"Do you know her name?" Cassie's heart pounded as she realized this might be the clue she had hoped for.

"Anna I think." Mirabel paused, then shook her head. "No, it was Emma. I remember, because I accidentally called her Emily once and she corrected me."

"Emma?" In her mind, Cassie ran through faces of the locals she'd met. No Emma surfaced. If she was a local she was sure that Mirabel would know her well. "Do you know where she lives?"

"All I know is that she's not from around here. She's not from Little Leaf Creek. I know everyone who lives in Little Leaf Creek. I heard her talking about being from Calhoon before, but I'm not sure if that's where she's living now, or where she grew up. Sebastian might know more. I've seen him with her before." Mirabel sighed. "I hope she doesn't take the news too hard."

"Do you still need me?" Cassie began pulling her apron off.

"No, the place will be dead, probably for the rest of the night, unless something new happens. I'm going to let Tamera run it for dinner and try to hunt down a lawyer that will take Aiden's case. So, we are prepared if this turns into a murder investigation." Mirabel tipped her head toward the door. "Go on, see what you can find out. Maybe you'll get lucky and crack the case."

"Okay, I'll let you know if I find out anything useful." Cassie headed out the door with her heart still racing.

CHAPTER 12

If what Mirabel said was correct, Cassie needed to speak to Emma. She had to find Emma. But how could she with only a first name and a possible town she lived in?

"Sebastian," Cassie murmured, as she reached her car. Mirabel mentioned that she had seen Emma talking to Sebastian. Even if Emma hadn't been Clyde's girlfriend, she might know something about him that would help solve his murder.

As Cassie drove toward Sebastian's house, she wondered how to strike up a conversation with him. When they worked together on the house it was easy. The subject matter was right in front of them. It didn't need to be personal or messy. It was all about hammers, nails, and spackle. But how did she ask him about a woman he might have dated without it getting awkward?

Cassie had to take the risk, if it meant finding Emma. She parked in the long, dirt driveway that led up to his ranch style house and held her breath at the sight of lights on in the living room and kitchen. What if he wasn't alone?

Cassie's heart dropped at the thought. She hated that it did. She shouldn't care at all if he wasn't alone. Yet, a pesky sense of dread welled up within her as she knocked on the door.

A few seconds after the knock, the door swung open.

"Cassie." Sebastian leaned against the doorway and smiled at her. "This is a nice surprise."

"Sorry to just come by." Cassie frowned as she realized she could have easily just called or texted him.

"Not at all, please come inside." Sebastian gestured for her to step past him.

Although Sebastian had been in her house quite often, she'd never been in his before. She noticed right away that it was all about function, without any splashes of color or design. It made her wonder how long he had lived alone, or if he just preferred a simplistic style.

"Can I get you a drink?"

"No thanks, I won't stay long." The well-worn couch and recliner set in the center of his spacious living room made her smile. He liked to hold onto things, it seemed.

"Oh, so you're here on business?" Sebastian slid his hands into the snug, worn pockets of his jeans as he gazed at her. "Out with it then."

"I just found out that there might have been someone in Clyde's life. Someone that he was close to." Cassie settled her gaze on his. "Someone that you might have been close to, as well."

"Oh?" Sebastian smiled slightly. "A name might make it easier."

"I only know a first name. Emma?" Cassie watched as he looked at her. "I think she lives in Calhoon."

"Emma?" Sebastian's voice wavered some as he spoke her name. "Sure, I know an Emma."

"At least one?" Cassie laughed.

"Not sure what that's supposed to mean." Sebastian drew his lips into a thin, tight line, then forced a smile. "But I do know an Emma from Calhoon."

Cassie's cheeks burned as she realized her attempt at a joke might have actually offended him.

"Well uh, Mirabel said she saw her with him a few times. If it's the same Emma. Anyway, I'm trying to find her. I think she might know more about what was going on with Clyde. Do you know her last name?" Cassie stared into his eyes.

"Do I know the last name of a woman I dated?" Sebastian quirked an eyebrow. "Just what do you think of me, Cassie?"

Cassie's voice caught in her throat before she could form any words.

"Alright." Sebastian chuckled. "We'll talk about that later. Emma Stratton. That's her name. I can't guarantee it's the same Emma, but it's likely. After we broke things off she did ask me about Clyde. She also does a bit of rock climbing. I gave her his number. But I never knew if anything came of it. She never told me. He never mentioned her to me."

"Maybe they thought it might upset you?" Cassie brushed her hair back over her shoulders as she took a breath and tried to regain her composure. "Maybe, make you jealous?"

"Oh no, it wasn't like that." Sebastian shook his head. "Emma and I were friends, then we dated a bit, now we're friends again. She's a good person, real hard working, real smart. I'm sure if she knows anything about Clyde she'll be happy to help you out."

"Do you think you could reach out to her? Maybe set up a meeting so we can talk about Clyde?" With each word Cassie spoke she felt more out of place. Was it wrong for her to use their friendship to pry into his ex-girlfriend's life?

"Of course, I can. I'll try to set something up for tomorrow." Sebastian grabbed his phone off of the kitchen counter. "Like I said, I'm sure she'll want to help."

"Thanks so much, Sebastian. I appreciate you doing this."

"Cassie, it's no trouble." Sebastian looked up from his phone, and straight at her. "Anything I can do to help, I'm happy to."

"Can you tell me about the dairy farm? The one with the trail that leads up to the cliffs? That's the way they think that Clyde went, right?"

"Most likely." Sebastian set his phone down again. "The guy who owns it, Nigel, he's real tough about who he lets on the property, but it's hard to monitor."

"Tough enough to decide to hurt Clyde for trespassing?" Cassie raised her eyebrows.

"That seems more than a little extreme to me. But I guess it's possible. I don't know the man well. He keeps to himself. I've heard a few people complain about him causing legal trouble for them, though." Sebastian glanced at his phone as it buzzed. "That's Emma. She said she'll meet us here for breakfast tomorrow before she starts work. Sound okay?" He glanced back at her.

"That won't put you out?" Cassie frowned.

"Not at all. I've been dying to impress you with my pancake-making skills." Sebastian's smile spread wide across his lips.

Cassie's heart fluttered as his gaze hung on hers. Could he really be interested in her as Tessa had claimed? She stared into his bright eyes, searching for the answer, and didn't realize that her silence had gone on too long, until he coughed and turned away.

"Unless of course you're gluten free or something. I can whip up something else."

"Pancakes are great. Thanks. I'll be here." Cassie turned back toward the door, her muscles tight from the tension that flowed through her.

"Good." Sebastian followed her to the door.

"See you tomorrow." Cassie hurried across the threshold and out onto the driveway. "Thanks again, Sebastian." She waved over her shoulder as she walked away.

CHAPTER 13

*A*s tempting as it was to go straight to Emma's house and try to find out what she could from her, Cassie knew that having her in a more relaxed environment with someone familiar might lead her to share more information. Instead, she drove back to her house, and as she parked in her driveway she felt a sense of urgency to update Tessa on everything that she had discovered. Not that any of it would necessarily lead in any particular direction, but it was something, and she knew she would be eager to hear about it.

Cassie patted the goats on the way inside and was halfway up the steps when Tessa's front door swung open.

"There you are." Tessa smiled as she held open the screen door. "I was wondering when you'd come by."

"Did you get a chance to talk to Shane?" Cassie stepped inside and let the door swing shut behind her. She bent down and rubbed behind Harry's ears.

"Yes, I did. He had something interesting to say, actually." Tessa led her into the kitchen. "But before we can get too far into this conversation, we need to eat." She pulled two plates down from a cabinet and dug two forks out of a drawer. Soon, they were across from each other at the table, with hefty slices of strawberry cheesecake in front of them.

"So, what did you find out about Shane?" Cassie dug her fork into her cheesecake. "Please tell me that he did it, and all of this can be over."

"Well, before I talked to him, I spoke with a few other people that indicated they had witnessed a wicked argument between him and Clyde. So, I thought we were definitely on the right track with Shane. I figured maybe he had gone up to the cliffs to have it out with Clyde again. But when I spoke to him, he told me a very different story." Tessa curled her upper lip. "Not that I necessarily believed a word of it."

"Tell me!" Cassie laughed as she gazed at her with a serious expression.

"Things like this can't just be told, I have to time it right." Tessa winked at her, then grinned. "So, according to Shane, the entire fight was staged."

"Staged?" Cassie gasped. "Are you kidding me? Why would they ever do something like that?"

"He said that ever since he and Clyde had come up with the idea of expanding Clyde's business into a full-fledged tourist adventure destination, they'd been getting pressure from their competition. Some of their rivals had even caused them to have trouble getting their licenses and permits set up. So, the two of them decided to make it look as if the business idea had blown up, that their partnership wasn't going to happen, just to take the heat and pressure off them long enough to get all of the business stuff taken care of, so that they could get it up and running. According to Shane, the fight was Clyde's idea, and it had gotten even more heated than they had rehearsed. It drew a lot more attention than they expected."

"Sounds a little fishy to me." Cassie savored another bite of the cheesecake. "I mean, it's a bit convenient to think that they just happened to stage this fight just a short time before Clyde was killed. I want to dig a bit more into it."

"Me too." Tessa narrowed her eyes. "So I did. I thought maybe he was putting me on. I decided I would try to verify if the business had stalled, or if they had continued to seek the permits they needed. I found one dated for the day before Clyde died, with both of their signatures on it. That indicates to me that Shane might have been telling the truth, at least about the partnership continuing. But it certainly doesn't rule him out as a suspect." She paused as she gazed at Cassie. "Now, it's your turn. I can tell you're about to burst. What did you find out?"

"You can tell that?" Cassie's eyes widened, as she wondered if she was really that easy to read.

"Just tell me." Tessa rolled her eyes.

"So, not only did Aiden claim that Clyde told him not to come up onto the mountain with him at all, but Mirabel told me that Clyde had been seeing someone. A woman named Emma who lives in Calhoon."

"That's not a lot to go on." Tessa frowned.

"No it's not, but luckily Sebastian just happens to know this woman." Cassie smiled.

"Why doesn't that surprise me?" Tessa chuckled.

"I don't think that man can walk into town without attracting attention. He's friends with everyone."

"Anyway, he was able to set up a meeting for tomorrow morning at his place. You should come with, he's making pancakes. I'm hoping that she's going to be able to tell me more about what Clyde might have been up to." Cassie looked into her eyes.

"So, Mirabel thinks this woman and Clyde were in a relationship?" Tessa sliced her fork down through her piece of cheesecake.

"Yes, and I tend to think she's right." Cassie put down her fork. "Or maybe I just hope she is. According to Mirabel, Clyde preferred to portray himself as single, but she said she saw Emma with him quite a bit."

"Well, let's hope he told her more than he told Shane. I asked him if Clyde has any other friends or girlfriends that might have something to say. He claimed that Clyde hadn't been seeing anyone. Fishy huh?" Tessa nodded.

"Real fishy. If the two were good friends and going into business together, why wouldn't Clyde have mentioned Emma? Mirabel said he liked to portray an image that he was single but he was still seen out with Emma. Surely Shane would know something about her." Cassie shook her head.

"Unless it just wasn't that serious. Or maybe they were just friends."

"It's possible." Tessa finished the last bite of her cheesecake. "I can tell you this much, we're not going to find out today. I think I'm going to read a book and get an early night, so I can make sure I don't miss out on Sebastian's pancakes. He's always trying to impress everyone with them."

Cassie smiled at the thought. So, maybe Sebastian wasn't interested in impressing her in particular, but either way she would be glad to have Tessa at her side during what she imagined might prove to be a rather awkward breakfast.

After Cassie said goodbye to Tessa and Harry, she walked back over to her house. But the moment she closed the door behind her, she realized that she wanted to do something. She didn't just want to sit around. She walked through the house, to the kitchen, and looked through the back window across Sebastian's field.

It was still light outside. She could go for a walk through the woods before it got dark. She could walk off some of that cheesecake. It was better than staying at home doing nothing. A little walk would clear her head and if she happened to come across the crime scene, so be it.

"It's a terrible idea." Cassie winced. There was no way to make her decision seem wise. But she also knew there was no way to talk herself out of it.

If Oliver got wind of what she was up to, she had no idea how he would react. She didn't intend him to find out. She grabbed a backpack and stocked it with a bottle of water and bug spray, then headed out through the back door.

With each step she took farther into the field, Cassie questioned whether she should turn back. What was even the point of doing this? What could she hope to find that the police hadn't uncovered? She wasn't a detective, that was for sure. But she did have a tendency to notice small things, sometimes overlooked things. She had been that way ever since she was a small child.

Just about everyone she'd spoken to lately had warned her to be careful, but there was a young man's future in the balance. If they didn't find who killed Clyde, Aiden might be the one to pay the price for his murder.

As Cassie picked her way through the brush and continued toward the woods, her anxiety grew. The woods were much darker than she expected. The terrain that had felt familiar enough when she was with Tessa, now looked far different. She pulled out her phone and looked up the video of Clyde that Trevor had shown her. It explained where he would be camping and climbing with Aiden. The coordinates were listed in the notes. She entered them into her GPS. It would at least get her close to where Clyde had set up camp. She plodded forward, despite her better judgment.

CHAPTER 14

*A*s Cassie looked ahead of her, she watched as the last light of the sun filtered through the trees. She turned the flashlight on her cell phone on, then trained the light on the trail ahead of her. She thought about turning back but she knew she was getting close.

The more Cassie walked, the more she wondered about her own sanity. She didn't have much hiking experience, and it hadn't occurred to her that Clyde might have chosen a rather difficult spot to set up camp. However, just as she was about to give up and turn back, she noticed some lights ahead of her. Her heart skipped a beat as she realized they were floodlights, likely set up by the police while the crime scene was investigated. Did that mean someone was still there?

Cassie crept forward as quietly as she could, but avoiding every twig and dried leaf on the ground proved impossible. By the time she stepped through the trees, she was certain that someone must have heard her coming. However, the well-lit crime scene appeared to be completely empty.

Cassie looked over the empty campsite. She could see a firepit that had been dug out. She presumed that was near where Clyde had set up camp. A pile of branches and kindling indicated that Clyde had done a lot of work gathering enough wood to keep himself warm. So, why would he put the stove in his tent? No possessions were scattered around the campsite. She guessed the items found had been bagged for evidence as the death was investigated.

As Cassie stepped farther into the crime scene she felt some apprehension. She knew that she had no right to be there. Although it wasn't roped off, she guessed that she was breaking at least one law just by being there. As she crept farther toward the edge of the firepit, the hair on the back of her neck stood up. This was near where Clyde had died, a man she had never met, but a man she knew to be full of life from the video she'd watched, and the description his friends gave of him.

Cassie believed that someone had killed him. Someone had gone to a lot of trouble to make it look like an accident, but in order to do that they had to be present at this campsite. Which meant, maybe they left something behind.

Cassie walked around the area. She had no idea what she expected to find there. If Oliver found out that she was there, she couldn't even imagine how he would react. She didn't want to. But she still couldn't turn back. She felt as if something pulled her to keep looking, something told her to continue to search, despite all of the good reasons she should turn back.

Cassie walked around the campsite thinking about what she knew about Clyde's murder. Clyde was camping alone, according to Aiden. He had chosen to be alone. But why? Why did his plans change at the last minute? Had something happened that made him need solitude? Or was he not alone at all?

How exhausted was Clyde after a day of climbing? He was used to the activity. She guessed he was in pristine physical shape if he was always active. Was he tired? Was he restless? Did someone wake him up? Did someone confront him before he even had the chance to lie down?

Was Clyde attacked? Was he lulled into a false sense of security? Did he know who his killer was? It crossed her mind that the killer still could have been a random passerby, but the likelihood of that was so slim she dismissed the thought. Instead, she knew that the people who would know where Clyde was, and how they could make his death look like an accident, were the people that knew him best, and one of them was most likely his murderer.

Cassie realized she was being ridiculous, there was no use being there, of course there would be nothing left behind. They had cleared the area out. A rush of disappointment washed over her. She had walked through the woods for nothing, and now she would have to walk back home in the dark. As she turned to leave, her foot caught on a tree branch laying on the ground and she stumbled forward toward the firepit. As she regained her balance her eyes cast over the firepit. Something caught her attention in the kindling beside it. It was shiny. She walked over to it.

Cassie knelt down to get a closer look. A small object lay wedged in the dirt. The area was well-lit, but she automatically trained the flashlight on her phone on it. The object looked so out of place amongst the leaves and wood. As she tugged it free, she felt its round, hard shape. She felt its slight weight.

"A ring?" Cassie let the object tumble into her palm and pointed her flashlight at it. The beam glinted off the solid gold surface and the gem that took up the middle of the piece of jewelry. Printed on either side of the stone were numbers. She recognized it as a class ring, and wondered if it might belong to the local high school. She didn't have too much time to think about it before a sound in the trees stole the breath from her lungs.

Cassie froze as she heard more leaves rustle. The air was still. She turned to see a figure coming out through the trees, toward her. Was she mistaken? No, the shadow on the ground confirmed that something was there. It was hard to tell exactly how close it was. But it wasn't hard to tell what it was. A person. Someone else who had decided to come out to the campsite after dark. Someone who knew that she shouldn't be there. Someone who, she guessed, could easily see her standing in the light. With trembling fingers she clung tightly to the ring in her hand and wondered if she should try to make a run for it. Would she even have a chance to escape? Was it the murderer returning to the scene of the crime? A random hiker that just happened to be by the crime scene? She hoped for the latter, but her heart pounded with the certainty that it might be the former.

Cassie started to back away slowly from the shadow. Should she call out? Should she run? Before she could make a decision, the shadow moved closer.

CHAPTER 15

Cassie held her breath, she tried not to make a sound. She turned slightly and realized she was close to the edge of the cliff. She couldn't move farther away from the person, there was nowhere to go. She froze where she stood.

"Whoever is there, you need to put your hands up!" The commanding voice carried through the mostly silent surroundings.

It coursed right down Cassie's spine as she recognized it instantly.

Cassie drew a slow breath in an attempt to calm herself down. There was no way to get away. She'd have to face him, hopefully before he decided to draw his weapon.

"It's me, Oliver." Cassie raised her hands and

forced herself to speak.

"Cassie?" Oliver stepped into the light and she could see him clearly now as he walked toward her. As soon as he reached her, his gray eyes locked to hers in the same moment that his jaw rippled.

"I'm sorry." Cassie gulped back another breath as he continued to stare at her.

"Just what do you think—" Oliver interrupted his own words as he cleared his throat. "I mean, why?" He shook his head. "Come out here, away from the edge. Come into the open."

The moment Cassie started to move, she realized her body had begun to shake. Was it when she saw the shadow, or when she heard his voice? As she stepped toward him he placed his hand on her shoulder.

"Cassie?" Oliver's grip softened as she continued to tremble. "Are you okay?"

"You startled me." Cassie's cheeks flushed as she looked away from him. "I didn't know who was out here."

"I'm sorry that I scared you." Oliver ran his hand soothingly along her shoulder, then sighed. "Not that I should be. Maybe a good scare is what you need to realize that you need to be more careful."

"Great, thanks. I'll keep that in mind." Cassie

crossed her arms, but didn't draw away from his touch. If he had hugged her, she probably would have burst into tears. She'd been so sure that she was going to have to fight for her life just moments before. As much as she hated to admit it, he was right. She'd put herself in a very dangerous position, and could only feel relieved that it was him and not Clyde's killer that was in the woods.

"I'm sorry." Oliver let his hand fall away as he gazed at her. "I had no idea it was you up here, otherwise I would have identified myself earlier. You know that, don't you?"

"Yes, of course." Cassie smiled slightly.

"What made you think that this was a good idea? What if it wasn't me that found you?" Oliver pursed his lips and looked up at the sky, then looked back at her.

"I just wanted to go for a walk, and once I started, I landed up here." Cassie continued to grip the ring tightly in her hand. "I know that Aiden is in a lot of trouble, and I know that there's still not a solid explanation for what happened to Clyde. I just thought if I could be in this space, maybe I'd figure something out."

"Oh?" Oliver stared straight into her eyes. "And did you?"

Cassie's heart raced as she tried to decide whether to tell him about the ring.

"You did, didn't you?" Oliver took a sharp breath before she could respond. "What did you find?"

Cassie held out her hand, her fingers red from holding them closed so tight. Slowly, she unfurled them and revealed the ring in her palm.

"I found it by the firepit."

Oliver remained silent as he studied the ring.

"I know I probably shouldn't have touched it. But I didn't know what it was at first. It was caught up in the kindling and buried near the firepit. Somehow it was missed, but I'm not surprised. It was well camouflaged by the leaves." Cassie looked up at him in the same moment that he looked up at her.

"Cassie, this is a good find." Oliver pulled a small plastic bag out of his pocket and scooped the ring into it. "Anyone could have left it here, but maybe it means something."

"Do you know if it is a class ring for the local high school?" Cassie watched as he peered at it through the plastic bag.

"Yes, it is, and from the year listed, it would be the year that Clyde graduated. It could be his." Oliver tucked the bag into his pocket. "I'm going to have to get it back to the station to have a closer look." He pointed his flashlight toward the trail, then looked back at her. "Let's go, I'll walk you back to your house."

"It's okay, I can make it on my own." Cassie started toward the trail.

"I'm sure you can." Oliver matched her pace. "But I'm not letting you out of my sight until I know that you're back at your house."

"Oliver, I really am sorry. I shouldn't have come up here." Cassie glanced over at him.

"No, you shouldn't have." Oliver looked over at her. "We should keep going before it gets too late."

"Do you really think that ring belongs to Clyde?" Cassie started walking.

"I think it's possible." Oliver stepped up beside her and matched her pace. "Hopefully, I will be able to find out for sure. There may be initials on it, or another way to track who purchased it."

"Good." Cassie felt some relief as they reached the end of the trail that led into Sebastian's field. "Did you know that Clyde had a girlfriend?"

"Emma?" Oliver followed just a step behind her. "How did you find out about her?"

"Mirabel. And Sebastian knows her."

"Oh." Oliver cleared his throat. "I've been looking into her, but I haven't had the chance to speak to her, yet. She hasn't returned my calls. Let me guess, she's an old girlfriend of Sebastian's?"

Cassie held her breath as she realized that maybe she had said more than she should have.

"Do you like pancakes?" Cassie met his eyes as it occurred to her that she didn't have much of a choice. If she didn't tell him about the meeting with Emma, he would find out about it soon enough. As the detective investigating the case, shouldn't he be invited?

"Sure." Oliver smiled as he continued past her in the direction of her house. "I've never been great at making them, but I do enjoy eating them."

"Well, Sebastian has set up a meeting with Emma for tomorrow morning." Cassie matched his pace as they neared her back porch. "It might be a good time for you to speak with her."

"A meeting?" Oliver paused beside her.

"He invited her over for breakfast. And me." Cassie gripped the railing of the porch as she studied him. "In such a relaxed setting she might be more willing to talk."

"Brilliant." Oliver nodded as he gazed at her. "I'll be there."

"Great." Cassie started up the steps.

"Cassie?" Oliver stepped up onto the bottom step,

but proceeded no farther.

"Yes?" Cassie glanced back over her shoulder at him. His narrowed eyes and tense jaw made her wonder if he was about to launch into the lecture that she expected to receive when he found her near the crime scene.

"I know this might not be the best timing. But I've learned in life, there's never really a perfect time." Oliver cleared his throat. "I mean." He lowered his eyes, then drew a slow breath. When he looked back up at her, the tension had been erased from his expression, replaced by a glimpse of fear and hope. The strong, determined man seemed a bit shy and nervous. "I'd like to take you to dinner sometime. If you would like that."

Cassie's eyes widened. She doubted that was the reaction he wanted, as his expression grew tense again.

Say something, Cassie, she ordered herself. But she couldn't manage to put two thoughts together.

"I'm sorry, forget I asked." Oliver laughed as he stepped back down. "It was a crazy idea."

"It's not crazy. I'd like that." The words popped out of Cassie's mouth before she could think them through. In fact, as she saw a smile spread across his lips, she wondered if she'd really spoken out loud.

"Great. Friday night? Or is that too soon?" Oliver ran his hand back through his hair. "Sorry, I don't really do this often."

"That's just fine." Cassie took a sharp breath as she wondered how she'd gotten to that moment.

"Great. See you in the morning." Oliver held her gaze a moment longer, then turned and walked around the side of the house.

Stunned, Cassie closed the door as she stepped inside. A part of her wanted to call him back and insist that she had made a mistake by agreeing to go out with him. She couldn't deny the fact that he'd been clear about his intentions. She'd promised herself that aspect of her life was over, she didn't want a relationship, she didn't want to date anyone, she wanted to be single, and yet when he asked, she hadn't said no.

Why had she agreed? She couldn't figure out the reasoning behind her decision. Yes, Oliver was intriguing, and she found him attractive, but she wasn't ready for another relationship. It's just two friends enjoying each other's company. Nothing more than that. It doesn't have to be a big deal.

Cassie continued to try to convince herself of that as she tossed and turned in her bed. By the time her alarm went off, she'd almost begun to believe it.

CHAPTER 16

*C*assie took a quick shower, dressed, then stepped out onto her porch.

"Good morning, neighbor." Tessa leaned against the fence their properties shared and smiled at her. "Ready to see what we can find out? Or would you rather tell me about you and Oliver on your back porch last night?"

"You saw us?" Cassie's eyes widened as she headed for her car.

"You know that Harry won't ever let me miss a beat." Tessa shook her head as she heard the dog give a sharp bark from inside of her house. "He started barking as soon as you two walked up. My question is, where were you coming from?"

"Get in. I'll tell you all about it." Cassie gestured for her to settle in the passenger seat.

"Maybe not all the details." Tessa chuckled as she sat down in the car.

"I went up to the woods after I left your house, yesterday." Cassie drove in the direction of Sebastian's house.

"By yourself?" Tessa swung her head to the side to look at her, her voice sharp.

"Yes, by myself." Cassie held up one hand. "I left when it was light. I couldn't relax, so I decided to go for a walk. I needed to walk off some of that cheesecake. I ended up at the crime scene. I didn't realize it would take me so long to get there and it would get dark so quickly. Trust me, I know it was a bad idea. But I did find something." As she filled her in about the ring she'd found, she noticed Tessa looked straight through the windshield. "Tessa, it was a good find."

"You shouldn't have gone up there. What if it was the murderer that found you?" Tessa shook her head.

"Tessa." Cassie sighed as she pulled into Sebastian's driveway. "I get it. I didn't think things through. But what do you think about the ring? Oliver said that it might belong to Clyde, but I'm not so sure. Why would it have been loose on the ground if it was his?"

"Well, it could have fallen off his finger, or maybe he took it off, or it could have easily belonged to a few other people, too, including Ron, Trevor's father." Tessa met her eyes as she turned the car off.

"I hadn't thought of that." Cassie frowned. "But you're absolutely right."

Tessa stepped out of the car, then stood back to allow Cassie to head up the walkway first.

Cassie braced herself as she knocked on the door. She knew that the morning would be full of surprises for Sebastian.

"Cassie!" Sebastian smiled as he opened the door. "Oh, and you brought Tessa?" He looked past Tessa, as Oliver walked up the driveway. "And Oliver?"

"I hope you don't mind." Cassie smiled. "I thought it would be best if Oliver heard whatever Emma has to say. He's been trying to contact her."

"I'm sure he has." Sebastian nodded at Oliver, then glanced over his shoulder into the house. "Emma, we have a bit more company than I had planned on. I hope that's okay with you."

"It's alright, Seby." A woman who looked to be in her early thirties stepped up behind him. Her blonde hair was piled high in a messy bun as she rested one hand on his shoulder and leaned past him to look at the others. "Ah, Detective Graham, why doesn't it surprise me that you ended up here?"

"I've been trying to reach you." Oliver shifted from one foot to the other. "I just have a few questions."

"Well, come inside and have some pancakes while you ask." Emma gave Sebastian a light slap on the shoulder. "Sebastian here makes the best pancakes around. I'm sure you know that already, Cassie. He loves making pancakes for his friends." She winked at her, then turned and walked back toward the kitchen.

Cassie's eyes widened at the comment. She felt Oliver's gaze heavy on her as she walked through the door, and hoped that maybe he hadn't heard Emma's words. No, she'd never had Sebastian's pancakes before, but clearly Emma had, plenty of times.

"I've got a few ready to go, but it won't take me long to whip up enough for everyone." Sebastian led them into the kitchen which featured a breakfast bar that wrapped around most of the large kitchen. "Take a seat. Emma, do you mind grabbing the syrup and butter?"

"Not at all." Emma showed no difficulty finding

the items despite there being many cabinets to choose from.

Cassie sat down at the breakfast bar. She felt some relief as Tessa sat down beside her.

Oliver continued to hover near the end of the bar.

"Emma, I want to say, I'm so sorry for your loss." Cassie watched as the young woman set the syrup and butter down on the counter.

"Thank you." Emma's voice softened. "I couldn't believe it when I first heard about it. And then, of course, I knew the idea that it was accidental is ridiculous." She looked over at Oliver. "I can't believe that you are even pursuing that theory."

"I'm exploring all avenues." Oliver leaned his hands against the bar as he looked into her eyes. "I'm sorry for your loss, Emma. I know it must be shocking to you. I don't want to cause you any more discomfort, it's just that if you want to help me to prove that this wasn't accidental and find out who did this, I'm going to need some information."

"Like what? That Clyde was an experienced mountain climber and camper that would never have that stove inside of his tent for any reason?" Emma raised her eyebrows. "That kind of information?"

"More like, who might have had a problem with Clyde. Who might have gone to all of the trouble to kill him and make it look like an accident. Was there anyone in his life that he was having trouble with? Was there anyone that had threatened him?" Oliver looked straight into Emma's eyes. "My impression is that you must have known about his current lifestyle the best. Am I wrong about that?"

"If you're asking me if we were seeing each other, then yes, you're right about that." Emma stared back at him. "I knew as much as Clyde was willing to let me know. As for enemies, I can't think of anyone that would want to hurt him. He was a generous, genuine man. He didn't play games. I'm sorry if that doesn't help."

"You say, he didn't play games, but wasn't keeping your relationship a secret a bit of a game?" Oliver's tone remained even, his expression unflinching, even as the others around him cringed in response to the direct question.

"He wasn't trying to hide me." Emma crossed her arms. "He's not the one that wanted it kept a secret. It was me."

"But why?" Cassie narrowed her eyes. "Was there something about Clyde that you were ashamed of?"

"Of course not." Emma pursed her lips, then

sighed. "My brother is involved in the adventure business, too. If he found out that I was dating Clyde, he would have been upset. He's very protective of me. When he saw the two of us together one day he warned me that I shouldn't get involved with him. He even warned me not to climb with him."

"I don't understand." Cassie shook her head. "Why would he care so much if you were involved with Clyde?"

"Clyde has a reputation in the business as being a big risk-taker, and also someone that doesn't like to settle down." Emma's cheeks reddened some. "Let's just say I have a bad habit of getting involved with guys that aren't looking for a serious relationship. We were going to tell him eventually, but not yet."

"So, you two had been together for a while?" Oliver pulled a notebook from his pocket.

"We're supposed to be having breakfast, remember?" Sebastian set a plate of pancakes down in front of Emma. "Let's not let this turn into an interrogation."

"It's okay, Seby." Emma picked up her fork and poked at the fluffy pancakes on her plate. "I'm not even sure if I can eat. It still doesn't seem real to me."

"It won't," Cassie whispered, as she reached out

to lightly pat Emma's hand. "It won't for a little while. Everything will just seem strange, as if it's not real, as if it's a dream."

"Exactly, that's exactly how it feels." Emma frowned. "We were only together for a few months, but it felt like a lot longer."

"I see." Oliver made a note, then tucked his notebook back into his pocket. "I appreciate your help, Emma. Contact me if you think of anything else please." He placed a card down in front of her.

"I will." Emma smiled slightly.

"Enjoy your pancakes." Oliver started to turn toward the door.

"I've got some for you, too, Ollie." Sebastian held out a plate to him.

"No thanks. I've got work to do." Oliver glanced between Cassie and Tessa, then continued out the door.

Cassie ate her pancakes as Sebastian and Emma discussed old times.

Tessa remained silent, steadily eating through her serving of pancakes, and some of the pancakes that Oliver had refused. Cassie grinned to herself. Tessa certainly had a big appetite and a sweet tooth. Although Tessa hadn't invited Sebastian into her home, it appeared that she didn't mind eating in his, if it helped an investigation.

"Thanks for joining us this morning, Emma." Sebastian set the last empty plate in the sink. "I know it couldn't have been easy for you."

"Actually, it's been nice." Emma smiled. "With so many people not knowing about our relationship, at least around you, I can be honest about how I'm feeling."

"Will you tell your brother soon?" Cassie looked into her eyes. "You shouldn't deal with this on your own."

"Maybe, I don't know." Emma sighed. "I just don't know how he would react."

Cassie watched as Emma turned to Sebastian for comfort. Sebastian's arms wrapped around her.

"I should get going. I have to get to work." Emma pulled away from him, then wiped at her eyes. "I'm glad there are so many people interested in figuring out what happened to Clyde. It would mean a lot to him."

"I'll walk you out." Sebastian followed her toward the door.

"Poor girl," Tessa muttered, the moment the pair were out of earshot. "She's going to be grieving

Clyde for a long time. They didn't have the chance to say goodbye."

"No, they didn't." Cassie pressed her hand against her chest. "I hope she can get through it." She thought of her own husband's death.

"She will." Tessa stood up. "The strength inside of us may come as a surprise, but it is always there when we need it."

Cassie frowned as she stood up from the bar stool and followed her to the door. She wasn't so sure she agreed with Tessa's sentiment, but she wished that it was true.

"Are you leaving?" Sebastian caught her at the door.

"Thanks for the pancakes." Cassie smiled at him as she pushed her hair behind her ear. "And for inviting Emma. I'm glad she has you to lean on."

"I wish I could do more." Sebastian looked down the driveway as her car pulled out of it. "Hopefully, her brother will be supportive."

"Do you know him well?" Cassie looked at him as he glanced away.

"A bit. He can be quite a hothead." Sebastian ran his hand along his right cheekbone.

"Are you speaking from experience?" Cassie watched as his hand drifted back down to his side.

"I've learned a few lessons along the way." Sebastian shook his head. "But one thing is certain, Patrick loves his sister. He would do anything to protect her."

"Interesting." Tessa cleared her throat. "Maybe he knew more about his sister's relationship with Clyde than he let on?"

"It's possible." Sebastian frowned. "He's a rough guy, but I can't see him killing Clyde."

"You said you don't know him well though, right?" Cassie stepped through the door. "It's worth looking into."

"Let me know if I can help." Sebastian leaned through the door and caught her hand before she could get too far away. "Go easy on Emma though, alright?"

"Of course." Cassie pulled her hand away. "I wouldn't do anything to upset her. Losing someone is hard enough."

"True." Sebastian met her eyes.

Cassie turned away and hurried to her car. It seemed to her that every time she made any progress in figuring out who might have had a problem with Clyde, the people around her were also digging into her own past.

CHAPTER 17

On the drive back to her house, Cassie noticed Tessa's silence.

"Are you okay?" Cassie looked over at her as she pulled into her driveway.

"We have a lot to discuss. Want to come over for a bit?" Tessa stepped out of the car.

"Sure." Cassie followed after her, but noticed that she didn't seem like herself. She was often quiet, but she seemed annoyed. "Tessa, what's going on?" She trailed after her as she headed for the kitchen.

"You should have told me that Oliver was going to be there. That was pretty tense." Tessa turned away from her as she grabbed a few dishes from the drainer and began putting them away.

"I didn't know it would be." Cassie frowned as

she watched her sharp movements. "I didn't know how to tell Oliver no, once he knew about the meeting with Emma. He's the active detective on the case. I thought it would be good for him to be there. It might help solve the murder."

"Maybe." Tessa turned back to face her. "But you had to know that involving him was going to make everything more difficult."

"Actually, that's the problem. I don't know. I don't know anything about him. All I know is that whenever I try to ask you anything about Oliver, you avoid the question, and the tension between the two of you is as thick as concrete. It's far worse than anything between Oliver and Sebastian." Cassie crossed her arms as she leaned back against the kitchen doorway. "I think it's time you tell me what the problem is between the two of you."

"You think so, huh?" Tessa closed a cabinet door harder than she needed to, then sighed.

"Yes, I do think so." Cassie crossed her arms. "I feel like I'm playing a guessing game when it comes to the two of you. Whatever happened, I think I should know about it."

"Look Cassie, Oliver and I were close. I've known him since he was born and I mentored him when he first became an officer. Even though we didn't work in the same jurisdiction at that time, we happened to get caught up in the same case." Tessa pulled out a chair at the kitchen table and sat down in it. "I've been keeping an eye on the kid since he was young and we both lived in Little Leaf Creek. I couldn't shake the need to continue to protect him."

"What happened?" Cassie sat down across from her. "Did something go wrong?"

"I trusted my instincts." Tessa clasped her hands together on top of the table. "It's the one thing I couldn't teach Oliver. No matter what I told him, he was always by the book. I warned him that sometimes you have to trust what you can't see, what you can't touch. Sometimes you just have to listen to your instincts when something feels wrong, or right." She looked down at the table. "He would argue the point with me, insisting that the best way to build a case was to be methodical, follow up every lead, move forward based on solid evidence, not on feelings. This case was a big drug bust. We were just there as back-up, to keep the undercover detectives safe during the raid." She sighed.

"Something went wrong?" Cassie asked.

"When we arrived at this big warehouse, something didn't feel right to me. The commanding officer sent Oliver one way, and me another." Tessa pressed her hand against her chest as she glanced up at her. "Watching him walk away felt like my heart was being torn from my chest. I don't know how else to explain it. I just knew, something was wrong. So, I disobeyed orders. I went after him, instead of going where I was told to. Within minutes, everything went sideways."

"Oh no." Cassie frowned.

"The dealers had been tipped off and arrived armed to the teeth. They started shooting, and Oliver was right in the middle of it all. I managed to get him to cover, but then we were pinned down." Tessa gave her leg a light slap. "That's when I was shot."

"Tessa, that must have been so difficult for you both." Cassie reached across the table and took her hand. "I'm sure that Oliver was grateful that you trusted your instincts."

"Not exactly." Tessa grimaced. "He blamed me for things going sideways. He said if I had followed orders, things would have gone down differently. He got angrier and angrier at me, and eventually it pushed us apart. He was quite angry at me for a long time. We've only recently gotten back to the point that we can even have a conversation." She shook her head. "He's stubborn if he isn't anything else."

"It seems like you two cared a lot about each other. Don't you think there's a way to work out what happened between you?" Cassie met her eyes.

"If there is, I haven't found it yet." Tessa sat back in her chair. "Sometimes, people just aren't meant to work it out, Cassie. Sometimes they just need to go their separate ways."

"But you can't, can you?" Cassie gazed at her with a faint smile. "You couldn't let him go that day, and you can't let him go now."

"Maybe not. But he can let me go, and that's what he wants to do. I have to respect that." Tessa stood up from the table. "So, if you think you can mend fences between us, please, don't bother."

"Maybe, I can't mend fences, but I could really use some advice." Cassie shifted in her chair as she wondered if it was a good idea to ask her.

"I am always happy to dispense some of my wisdom." Tessa grinned at her as she leaned on the back of her chair.

"It's about Oliver." Cassie coughed, then took a deep breath. "He asked me to dinner."

"He did?" Tessa's grin spread even wider. "Well, I didn't think he had it in him. I guess he decided that he had to step up before Sebastian did."

"I'm not sure about any of that." Cassie frowned.

"I hope you let him down easy. His heart already has too many scars." Tessa winced.

"That's the thing. I said yes." Cassie shook her head. "I have no idea why, but I said yes. Now, I'm wondering if I've made a terrible mistake. What do you think?"

"I think Oliver is a wonderful man, and you're safer with him than you are with anyone else on this earth." Tessa sighed. "But I also think you should know he's not the easiest man. He isn't like Sebastian. He doesn't take life in his stride. He doesn't date often. When he does, he takes it very seriously. I wouldn't want him to get hurt."

"So, I should cancel?" Cassie held her breath.

"That depends." Tessa looked straight into her eyes. "What do your instincts tell you?"

Cassie stared back at her as the question rolled through her mind. What did her instincts tell her? She clenched her jaw as an answer surfaced very clearly. Run, run as fast as you can.

She'd been through one marriage, and one loss, and that was enough for her. She couldn't bear the thought of losing someone else.

"I think we should track down Emma's brother and speak to him. If he's as protective as she claims, maybe he found out something about Clyde that made him snap." Cassie stood up from the table. "I'll see if I can find out a bit more about him while I'm at the diner today. Mirabel didn't seem to know much about Emma, but one of the other waitresses might know something about her and her brother."

"Good luck." Tessa watched as she walked toward the door. "With the investigating, and with the avoidance."

"Clever Tessa, so clever!" Cassie waved over her shoulder as Harry gave a playful bark.

CHAPTER 18

*A*s Cassie stepped through the door of the diner, she was more determined than ever to try to help find out what happened to Clyde.

Cassie still felt that whoever killed Clyde had to know him well. The killer had to be able to get close enough for Clyde to be vulnerable. The killer probably knew that Clyde would be alone, despite the fact that he disclosed his plans to climb with Aiden. Although she hadn't completely ruled Aiden out as the killer, she felt he was very low on the list. He had no motive that she could think of, and a lot of family and community support. Still, she couldn't let that completely sway her.

"Good morning, Mirabel." Cassie picked up her apron as she smiled at the woman behind the counter. Her tightly braided hair sparkled in the early morning sunlight, catching the hints of blonde that filtered through the auburn strands. "Has it been busy, yet?"

"Not too bad." Mirabel flashed Cassie a brief smile, then paused and gazed at her. "Cassie?"

"What?" Cassie pulled the apron on.

"Something is different about you." Mirabel narrowed her eyes.

"I don't think so." Cassie smoothed her dark brown curls back into a ponytail and wrapped a hairband around it.

"Are you sure?" Mirabel tipped her head to the side. "You've got a glow about you."

"A glow?" Cassie laughed. "It must be Sebastian's pancakes. I had some this morning."

"What?" Mirabel almost dropped the coffee pot she held in one hand.

"Careful!" Cassie frowned as she took the pot from her and set it on the burner. "Are you okay, Mirabel?"

"I'm just surprised that you got to have Sebastian's pancakes so soon. He must like you, I knew he did, though. He's only ever made them for me twice in all this time." Mirabel laughed. "They are delicious."

"Mirabel!" Cassie laughed as well and shook her head. "I don't think so, I think he must like Emma. Her name is Emma Stratton, and she was there, along with Tessa, and Oliver!"

"Wow, what a crew." Mirabel pursed her lips. "How did things go with Emma? Did she tell you if she was dating Clyde?" She wiped down the counter but kept glancing over at her.

"She did. She said she wanted to keep it a secret because her brother is super overprotective. You don't happen to know him, do you?" Cassie walked over to the sugar dispensers and began to fill them.

"No." Mirabel shook her head and pointed toward the door. "But Avery might, she grew up in Calhoon."

"Oh." Cassie looked at the door as Avery and her friend Karen, from the historical society, walked into the diner. She wasn't sure how to ask Avery about Emma's brother, they didn't know each other very well.

Avery and Karen waved hello, walked straight over to the counter and sat down in front of them.

"Hi, ladies. Good to see you." Mirabel smiled. "Your usual?"

"Yes please." They replied in unison.

As Cassie got their order together, Mirabel leaned over the counter.

"We actually wanted to ask you something." Mirabel looked at Avery as Cassie listened closely to the conversation.

"Sure." Avery shrugged.

"Do you know anything about Emma Stratton's brother? I heard he's very protective of Emma?" Mirabel asked. Cassie realized that Mirabel would take care of the dilemma of how to broach the subject for her.

"Yes, Patrick. I used to see him around. He is very protective of her. They lost their mother pretty young, and their dad was around enough to give them food and shelter, but that was about it. Patrick took taking care of his sister pretty seriously, even though he's actually a few years younger than her. They always looked after each other. They are very close. They have the same interests. Work at the same place." Avery frowned, but seemed happy to offer some gossip. "I could see why he'd be upset if he found out that she was dating Clyde. Clyde's not known for being very stable. Clyde also had some issues with Emma and Patrick's boss, Devin Blight from Adventures Aplenty."

"Oh?" Cassie remembered meeting him outside

the police station. She poured Avery, Karen, Mirabel and herself a cup of coffee from the fresh pot and started another.

"That's right I heard about that. Devin doesn't come around here much, he's also from Calhoon. But he and Clyde clashed a few times. I guess they consider each other competition since they're both in the adventure business." Mirabel shrugged. "I can't imagine getting into a throwdown with Tammy who runs the diner over in Sweedesboro, but I guess that's a little different."

"I guess." Cassie took a sip of her coffee. "It seems to me that Clyde only took his work seriously, and not much else in his life. Was he that way in high school, too?"

"He was a bit more responsible then. He was a jock for sure, but he didn't really spend too much time with them. He preferred to be enjoying nature." Mirabel greeted a customer who stepped into the diner. "Be right over with a cup of coffee, Cheryl."

"What about other people in his graduating class? Did he have any friends or enemies back then? Anyone that stands out to you?" Cassie poured a cup of coffee for Cheryl and handed it over to Mirabel.

"Let me think about that for a few minutes."

Mirabel walked over to the customer with the cup of coffee.

As Cassie continued to fill what needed to be filled, her thoughts traveled back to Oliver, despite her best efforts to avoid it. She was relieved when a customer distracted her from it all, until she looked into Ron's eyes.

"Oh, it's you." Ron settled at the bar and sighed. "I guess it shouldn't surprise me."

"Coffee?" Cassie swallowed back her surprise at his presence and turned to grab a pot from the burner.

"Please. Lots of it." Ron rubbed his hand across his eyes. "I've just come from what felt like an hours long interrogation with the local detective." He took the cup of coffee from her and splashed some cream into it. "That man really needs a vacation."

"Sounds like it." Cassie tipped her head toward his hand. "What happened?" His knuckles were bruised, as if he had been in a fight.

"Oh this?" Ron shook his head. "Drunken bar fight." He winced as he lightly touched the bruise with his other hand. "Another one of my great decisions. But what can I say, my only talent is getting into trouble."

"Maybe if you took a little time to settle down,

things would calm down around you." Cassie noted a white band on his finger as he picked up his cup of coffee. "Divorced?" She pointed out the pale skin.

"Ha, no. That's one mistake I never made." Ron chuckled. "Just misplaced my ring." He scratched the back of his neck. "Not sure where."

"Maybe when you were hanging out with Clyde?" Cassie pushed the sugar dish toward him.

"Oh, now you're the one asking the questions, huh?" Ron narrowed his eyes. "Take your best shot. I'm not going to confess to anything I didn't do."

"Sometimes when we have a little too much to drink we do things that we never expect are possible." Cassie raised her eyebrows. "I'm sure you and Clyde have shared a drink or two."

"No, we haven't." Ron glared at her. "Can I drink my coffee in peace?"

"Of course." Cassie forced a smile, then walked over to another customer who had settled at the counter. When she turned back, she saw Ron's empty seat, and his empty coffee cup, but no payment or tip. She sighed as she gathered the cup and placed it in the sink.

"You know, there is one other person I can remember Clyde spending some time with when we were all in high school. His name is Justin. Justin

Traller, if I remember correctly." Mirabel laughed. "It's been years." Her laughter faded as she briefly closed her eyes. "It's always shocking how fast time goes by."

"Yes, it is."

A parade of customers came through the diner, but Cassie's mind focused on the name that Mirabel gave her. Clyde's friend, Justin Traller. Any chance she got between customers she looked up information about him. By the end of her shift she knew his address and his workplace. She also knew that he was friends on social media with Emma's brother, Patrick. Could it just be a coincidence that the two were connected?

CHAPTER 19

Cassie found Tessa in her backyard feeding her goats, Billy and Gerry. She smiled at the sight of it. She never expected her neighbor to have goats. It was something she never would have witnessed during her many years of living in the city. Moving back into small town life had been refreshing, however it hadn't allowed her to leave everything behind as she had hoped. At least not yet.

"Cassie, how'd it go at the diner?" Tessa offered her some feed from the bag beside her.

"Thanks." Cassie filled her palms with the food, then watched as Tessa continued to feed the hungry goats. "I saw Ron at the diner." She raised her eyebrows. "He has a tan line on one of his fingers and no ring, but I don't know for sure if it's from his class ring."

"Interesting. Did you ask him?" Tessa glanced over at her.

"He said he'd lost his ring. I didn't push it too far, but he was fresh out of an interrogation with Oliver. Maybe he got something out of him. He seemed pretty sketchy, though." Cassie patted Billy, the white goat.

"Do you like him for Clyde's murder?" Tessa briefly met her eyes before she looked back at the goats.

"Maybe. I don't know why, but I just can't shake the idea that we need to find out more about Emma." Cassie held out her hand to the goats, who eagerly snapped some of the feed out of her palm.

"What makes you think that? There has to be something driving the feeling." Tessa reached out and gave each of the goats a stroke along their back. "Good boys. Don't take any fingers off."

Cassie drew her hand back with a faint frown. She hadn't known her fingers were at risk to begin with. Was Tessa joking with her?

"I think it's because Clyde canceled his plans with Aiden at the last minute. They had planned this trip for some time, and I know Aiden was really excited about it. So, what would make someone cancel their plans at the last minute?" Cassie looked up at Tessa and smiled. "Who would you have canceled your plans for?"

"Ah, I see." Tessa raised her eyebrows. "You think it was for Emma?"

"Maybe Emma decided that she wanted to join him on his adventure. She is also into rock climbing. Clyde didn't want a kid around to interfere with his romance, so he canceled his plans with Aiden." Cassie looked over at her. "What do you think?"

"It makes sense, you're right." Tessa tossed a bit more feed on the ground for the goats.

"But that means that Emma would have been there with Clyde, even though she didn't mention that to us this morning." Cassie took a deep breath. "And it also means that she might be the killer that we're looking for. It's hard for me to believe that she would have done that, though."

"Everyone is a possible suspect." Tessa narrowed her eyes. "My time on the police force has shown me that all avenues must be investigated."

"So, what do you think Emma's motive could be?" Cassie kicked her foot through the loose soil near the fence, then leaned back against it, the weight of the possibility of Emma being a murderer shocked her. She recalled the way Emma smiled at Sebastian. Her chest tightened with fear at the thought of him being in danger. Her cheeks flushed and her heart skipped a beat. What was that? She couldn't focus on it long before Tessa's voice drew her focus back to her.

"Jealousy. Betrayal." Tessa glanced over at her.

"It's possible." Cassie patted Gerry. "Maybe Emma saw Clyde with someone else? Or she could have even gotten angry that he planned to spend time with Aiden instead of her?"

"We know that Clyde was keeping his relationship with Emma under wraps. Emma claims it was because of her brother, but we don't know that for sure." Tessa smiled. "Maybe if we find out more about their relationship, we'll be able to stir up a proper motive for Emma to kill him. That's assuming she was even there in the first place."

"I definitely think it's worth looking into. Mirabel said that from what she knew Clyde was usually single. It was unusual for him to date someone. I'd say there was probably a reason for that. Maybe he's had some troublesome relationships in the past. Or maybe he felt pressured to be free, as part of his adventurous lifestyle. But clearly he changed his mind when it came to Emma."

Cassie stared off across Sebastian's field as she considered it. "I wonder if Emma was telling the truth about it being her idea to keep it a secret. Maybe Patrick, her brother, can offer some insight into what was happening between them. She said she was trying to keep the relationship a secret from him, but maybe he knows something about it."

"That might be a good place to start. Let's see if Patrick has anything to say about Clyde." Tessa nodded. "But we'll have to tread carefully. We don't want to get Emma into trouble."

"I also found a connection between Clyde and Patrick. Patrick works in the adventure business as well. Maybe they knew each other through their work. So, we don't have to bring Emma into the conversation straight away. If Patrick doesn't give us anything, Justin might. I saw that Patrick and Justin are friends on social media." Cassie pulled out her phone and selected the address that she'd found earlier in the day. "Patrick doesn't live too far from here. Up for a road trip?"

"Sure. Just let me check in on Harry and I'll meet you at your car." Tessa headed for the house.

Cassie watched her go. She noticed her limp, and now knew what had caused it. She had taken a bullet to protect Oliver, and Oliver turned his back on her?

What kind of person did that? The thought made her uneasy. She knew there were always two sides to a story, but Tessa's version didn't leave much room for debate on what happened. If she did go to dinner with Oliver, she intended to try to find out more.

CHAPTER 20

As Cassie waited for Tessa in her car, her phone buzzed with a text. She smiled at the sight of Sebastian's name, and the inquiry that followed. He was eager to help her with the repairs on the house, but she'd been so busy caught up with trying to help find the murderer that she hadn't been available.

Cassie sent him a quick text back putting him off for another day and wondered if he would get frustrated. He seemed like the type of person that couldn't be flustered easily.

"Sebastian, huh?" Tessa grinned as she opened the passenger side door.

"Were you spying on me?" Cassie slid her phone

into the holder on her dashboard and closed out her texts.

"It's my nature." Tessa buckled her seat belt then looked over at her. "I'm not trying to tell you what to do here, but it might be a good idea to pick one or the other before they come to blows over you."

Cassie started the car and stared hard through the windshield. "How about neither?"

"Cassie, are you okay?" Tessa's tone softened as she watched her navigate the streets.

"Yes." Cassie tried to focus on the directions the phone gave her. "I just never pictured anything like this, and I'm not sure that it's something I want."

"Don't let anyone pressure you into something you don't want." Tessa shook her head. "But you also can't let fear keep you away from something that you do."

"Can we just talk about Clyde?" Cassie glanced over at her, then turned down a street that led toward Patrick's house.

"Sure." Tessa cleared her throat. "So, we know that Clyde canceled his plans with Aiden."

"If we believe Aiden." Cassie frowned. "Which my instincts tell me to."

"Right, but without proof of where he was at the

time, then we can't completely rule him out. Or the two guys we found on the mountain." Tessa tapped her fingertips on the dashboard. "Although, I think that Oliver would have gotten evidence and maybe even a confession out of them by now if they had done it. My guess is they would have been pretty sloppy about it."

"Oliver." Cassie rolled her eyes. "He's still not even investigating this as a murder."

"Because there's no evidence that a murder took place. But just because he hasn't officially called it a homicide doesn't mean he isn't investigating it as one." Tessa leaned her head back against her seat.

Cassie parked in the street in front of Patrick's house and eyed the car in the driveway.

"I'm pretty sure that's his, so he's probably home."

"He might not be interested in talking to us, though." Tessa popped the passenger side door open. "Let's see what we can find out."

Cassie followed her up the driveway. She noticed rows of flowers on either side of the driveway and recalled that she was supposed to be planning the garden with Sebastian. It would have to wait. As she neared the front door, the elaborate landscaping around the house drew her attention.

"Someone put a lot of work in here." Cassie paused just behind Tessa as she knocked on the door.

Seconds later the door swung open to reveal a man she guessed to be about the same age as Emma, maybe a little younger.

"Patrick?" Cassie spoke up from behind Tessa.

"Yes?" Patrick narrowed his eyes. "This isn't some sales thing, is it?"

"No, not at all." Tessa stepped forward. "We know that you work at Adventures Aplenty and we wanted to speak to you about Clyde Timpson's death."

Cassie held her breath as she wondered if Patrick would turn them away.

"And?" Patrick pushed the screen door open and stepped outside. "What about it?"

"It's just that we believe that Clyde's death wasn't an accident." Cassie folded her hands in front of her and studied him as she continued in the calmest tone that she could muster. "We believe that he was murdered. We're wondering if you might have an idea of what happened to him?"

"Me?" Patrick glared at her. "All I know is that he had it coming?"

"What do you mean?" Cassie asked.

"Look, he should have left my sister alone." Patrick scowled.

Cassie was relieved that he had mentioned Emma first, so she wouldn't have to.

"Where was Emma on the night Clyde died?" Cassie decided to try and get as much information out of him as possible. Tessa glanced over at her with a faint nod of reassurance.

"How should I know?" Patrick glowered. "I don't keep track of where my sister is."

"Really? So, you don't know if she was with Clyde?" Cassie met his eyes. "It seems like you care a lot about her, but you don't care who she dates?"

"Look, my relationship with Emma is complicated. We pretty much only had each other growing up. I'm trying to give her a little space because she thinks I'm too controlling." Patrick rolled his eyes.

"But you still know where she was, don't you?" Tessa stared straight at him. "You know exactly where she was, or where she was supposed to be."

"Look, all I know is that she told me that she was going with a group of girls to some spa retreat thing. But then a friend of hers told me that she didn't go." Patrick frowned as he looked between them.

"So where was she?" Tessa took a slight step forward.

"I went to check for her at her house but she wasn't there. I knew where Clyde was camping, and I was about to go look for her there to try and make sure she was okay. But as I was leaving her house, she came home with Janice, a friend of hers. They had been out shopping and were just stopping at home to get changed and go out to get something to eat. Janice was going to stay at Emma's house overnight. Janice's boyfriend had just broken up with her, so Emma had cancelled her plans so she could be with her. She wasn't with Clyde. The police spoke to Janice and they know where Emma was, that's all that matters." Patrick held up his hands. "I don't have anything else to say. If you want to know more, you're going to have to ask Emma." He stepped back into the house and closed the door.

"Well, that didn't go too well." Cassie frowned. "We really didn't find out anything."

"Actually, it went great." Tessa led the way back to the car. "We know that Emma was with a friend when Clyde was murdered, which according to Patrick the police have verified. So, we can look into that more. And we also know one other thing." She opened the passenger side door then paused to look over the top of the car at her. Tessa squinted as sun reflected off the top of it. "Patrick really is obsessed with protecting his sister. Maybe he is lying and he did actually go look for her at the campsite."

"Even if Emma wasn't there, Patrick might have been." Cassie's eyes widened at the thought. "But Patrick didn't go to the same high school as Clyde, he wouldn't have had a class ring."

"That ring might have been Clyde's." Tessa settled into the car.

As Cassie sat in the driver's seat and turned the car on, she looked over at Tessa. "There's one other person who might be able to tell us more. Clyde's friend from high school that Mirabel mentioned, Justin Traller. My guess is that he's at work right now."

"Let's go have a conversation with him then. I remember his family moved to Little Leaf Creek and he lived here for a few years when he was in school, I doubt he remembers me, though. He had a climbing accident a few years back. I wasn't living in Little Leaf Creek at the time and I don't remember exactly what happened. But he was climbing with a friend and his friend died." Tessa settled back in her seat.

"We're getting closer, I can feel it." She squeezed her hands into fists, then relaxed them.

Cassie could easily imagine Tessa as a young officer, just starting out, determined to find the truth. It appeared as if she still had that same dedication and determination inside of her.

CHAPTER 21

As Cassie drove to Freemar Sports and More, the sports store that Justin had listed on his social media as his current workplace, she hoped that they would be able to find out something more from him. It was a bit of a long shot, but it was worth a try.

Cassie parked near the front of the store which didn't look too busy. The middle of the day wasn't a common time for most people to shop.

Tessa pulled open the glass door, then pointed out the camping equipment along one wall.

"This looks like a place where Clyde would spend some time."

"It does." Cassie nodded as she scanned the store for any sign of Justin. She found him stocking a shelf with basketballs in the corner of the store. "There he is. How are we going to get him to talk to us?"

"I have an idea." Tessa pulled her phone from her pocket as she walked in Justin's direction. "I just can't believe it. I'm just so shocked that this happened." She shook her head as she paused not far from Justin. "It just breaks my heart."

"Is there something I can help you with?" Justin turned around to face Tessa, just as she held up her phone to show Cassie a video of a news report about Clyde's death that had been posted.

"It's just tragic," Cassie murmured, as she shook her head.

"Shedding tears over that guy?" Justin pursed his lips as he looked away from the video. "Trust me, that's a waste of your time."

"How can you say that?" Tessa looked up from the video. "He was so talented, so brave."

"Sure, talented and brave." Justin crossed his arms. "That guy wasn't so great. I knew him in high school, and I can tell you the truth about him if you want to hear it."

"Sure." Cassie offered a small smile. "I always like to know the truth."

"Did you really know him?" Tessa's eyes widened.

"I did." Justin grabbed his phone from his pocket,

thumbed across the screen for a moment, then held up a picture of himself and Clyde on the side of a mountain. They both looked to be in their late teens. "Does that prove my story?"

"I think so." Cassie nodded as she gazed at the picture. Her heart pounded as she wondered how the two men had gone from being friends to Justin practically saying that he deserved to die. "But if you two were friends, how could you be so casual about his death?"

"We were friends. When we were in high school, we used to climb a lot together. We even entered into a few competitions as a team. We planned to do a lot more competitions together." Justin tucked his phone back into his pocket. "But then he decided he wanted to go a different way. He got into rescue climbing."

"That sounds like a noble thing to do." Tessa shrugged. "He wanted to save people. What's so wrong with that?"

"He didn't just want to save people. He wanted to be the best at saving people." Justin sighed, then clicked his tongue against his teeth. "That guy, he was all about ego. He had to be the best at everything. He wanted his name in the newspaper and all over the internet, and he would do anything to make sure that it was."

"Sounds like he liked the attention." Cassie crossed her arms as she studied Justin. Was he just jealous that Clyde had done better in the climbing world than he had? "What about you? Why didn't you go into the same field?"

"I wanted to be a mountain climber. I wanted to conquer the tallest mountains. I had my entire future planned around it. But Clyde changed all of that." Justin held up one of his arms. "You can't see it but my arm is full of pins and hardware."

"You had an accident?" Tessa's eyes narrowed, as she studied the scars on Justin's arm.

"Had an accident? You could say that. My new climbing partner and I were practicing for a big competition. We were doing just fine, until some bad weather hit. The mountain got slippery fast and we couldn't go up or down. We were stuck on a ledge way high up. But I told my buddy Alex not to worry. I contacted the rescue team, and I assured him that Clyde would be on it, and we would be safe in no time." Justin's upper lip curled as he looked away from them both.

"That's not how it played out?" Tessa's gentle prompting drew Justin's gaze back to her.

"No, it wasn't. Clyde showed up with something

to prove. He didn't take the precautions he needed to, and when he tried to rescue my friend, my friend slipped. He didn't secure him well enough. I tried to catch him, I had him for a minute." Justin ran his hand down along his scarred arm. "The weight, the velocity, it tore my arm apart. I couldn't hold on." He winced as he took a sharp breath. "All Clyde had to do was take the time to make sure that everything was secure. He just had to do his job right, but he didn't. He was too busy showing off, and it cost my friend his life. So, if you expect me to cry for a guy like that, no, sorry. It's not going to happen."

Cassie's eyes settled on his hand which still clung to his injured arm, then she looked at the other hand that hung by his side. She looked for a ring on his fingers. But he wasn't wearing one, and she couldn't see any sign of a tan line to indicate that he usually did wear one. But by his own admission he had plenty of motive to want to go after Clyde.

"Did you tell that story to Patrick Stratton, Emma's brother, when you found out that Emma was dating Clyde?"

"He's my friend, of course I did." Justin shrugged. "He found out his sister had been spending some time with the guy and knew I went to school with him and used to climb with him, so he asked me about him. I told him the truth. I told him that he should keep Emma as far away from Clyde as he could, especially if they were by the cliffs." Justin looked from Cassie to Tessa. "You can admire whoever you want, just don't expect me to shed a tear over a man who didn't value anyone's life but his own. Now, did you actually want to buy something?"

"I'll take one of these." Cassie grabbed a basketball from the shelf.

"Good choice." Justin walked with her over to the register.

"Do you think maybe he just made a mistake?" Tessa watched as he rung up the basketball. "That can happen. You said yourself the weather was bad."

"Mistakes can happen. But not when you're trained to save lives. He cut corners and took a chance that he shouldn't have." Justin met Tessa's eyes. "That's not a mistake. That's murder in my eyes."

Cassie took the basketball from him, then turned toward the door. His words played through her mind. As soon as they were outside, she turned to look at Tessa.

"If he believes that Clyde practically murdered

his friend, then maybe he decided it was time to even the score."

"Or maybe, Patrick didn't want Clyde taking the same risks with his sister, and decided to eliminate the problem. I remember that fatality though, and I don't think it was Clyde's fault, the conditions were treacherous." Tessa opened the passenger door of the car. "I'd say both Patrick and Justin had motive, but we still need to figure out if they both had the opportunity."

As Cassie drove back toward her house, she ran through the possibilities in her mind. Maybe Clyde had canceled his climb with Aiden because he wanted to be alone. Maybe he'd done it because he wanted to be with Emma. Or maybe he'd done it because his old friend Justin decided to give him a call to get together.

"I wish we could get into Clyde's phone records. That might tell us a lot." Cassie frowned. "I doubt that Oliver would be willing to share that information with us."

"No, he wouldn't. But luckily, I have a few friends who don't mind doing me favors." Tessa pointed out Sebastian's blue pickup truck as Cassie pulled into her driveway. "It looks like you have company. I'll let you know what I find out."

CHAPTER 22

Cassie braced herself as she approached the front door of her house. She guessed that Sebastian might be more than a little annoyed with her, and he had good reason. They had made plans together to fix up the house and get it to where she wanted it to be. But those plans had gone by the wayside the moment that Clyde turned up dead.

She opened her front door and peeked inside. "Sebastian?"

When Cassie received no answer she continued on farther into the house. Everything remained quiet, with no hint of Sebastian being around. As she reached the back door that opened off the kitchen into the backyard she caught sight of him bent over the space that they intended to turn into a flower garden. His shirtless back glistened with sweat as the sun played off of it. She noted his t-shirt tossed into the grass not far from him and guessed that he had been working for quite some time.

"Hi!" Cassie called out as Sebastian suddenly looked up at her.

"Hey." Sebastian wiped his forearm across his forehead, then leaned on the shovel. "Sorry, I probably should have let you know I'd be doing this."

"Please, don't apologize." Cassie smiled. "I should be the one that apologizes, I know I've been out of touch about all of this."

"It's no problem." Sebastian dug the shovel a bit deeper into the soil. "I think I know what you want." He glanced up and met her eyes in the same moment that his smooth accent delivered those words.

He's talking about the garden, Cassie.

"It's the perfect spot." Cassie turned her attention to the space he'd begun turning over. "It will get plenty of sun."

"Not as much as the front yard, but that will be good for some of the things that you want to plant." Sebastian tipped his head toward a space near the back porch. "I thought a small water feature might look good there, if that's something you'd like. I probably have one laying around."

"You have everything, don't you?" Cassie glanced up at him and smiled.

"Not everything." Sebastian held her gaze. "I collect things when I help people out. You'd be surprised at the perfectly good stuff that people will just throw away, just because they don't like the look of it." He brushed a few strands of his hair away from his forehead. "Or maybe they can't see the potential in it."

"But you do." Cassie turned toward the house. "You must be roasting, it's such a warm day for the end of summer. Let me get you a drink."

"Sure, water would be best." Sebastian coughed.

Cassie blushed as she recalled her disaster of an attempt to make lemonade.

"I'll be right back."

Cassie headed into the house and filled a glass with ice and water. As she looked through the back window at Sebastian digging into the soil again, she wondered if there was some truth to what Tessa said. It seemed to her that Sebastian was friendly with almost everyone. He was just a very warm and open person, that was probably what Tessa sensed. That he took an interest in everyone. Whether or not he was interested in her as more than just friends, she valued his friendship more than anything and hoped that it would continue.

Cassie returned to his side with the glass.

"Thanks so much." Sebastian took the glass and began to gulp the liquid down. As he took a breath he looked over at her. "How's the investigation going? Did you figure it all out, yet?"

"Not yet." Cassie frowned. "But maybe we're a little closer. Sebastian, how well do you know Emma?"

"Pretty well. Like I said, we're friends. We went on a couple of dates." Sebastian lowered the glass as he studied her. "Why?"

"Tessa and I spoke to her brother today, and a friend of his. Both had some really terrible things to say about Clyde." Cassie slipped her hands into her pockets. "I'm just wondering if you thought they might have had something to do with all of this."

"Like I said, her brother's a little crazy." Sebastian finished the last sip of the water, the ice cubes still nearly fully frozen as they clinked against the empty glass. "He threatened me after I took her out on one date. He doesn't get it, she's her own person." He licked a bit of the water from his lips. "Like everyone, she should be able to date whoever she pleases, right?"

"Right." Cassie nodded as he met her eyes.

"Anyway, I can't say whether he would be involved. I mean I can't see him killing Clyde, but I guess if he thought Emma was in trouble, maybe. But if you're talking about his friend Justin, that guy, I could see him definitely being angry enough to do something. I went to Patrick's workplace once to buy something. It was before Emma started working there. Justin was there with Patrick, they were chatting. While I waited, Clyde came in. Justin started to go off at him, and the owner of the place, Devin, threw him out. It was a little crazy." Sebastian frowned. "I hadn't thought about that until now, it was quite some time ago."

"Interesting." Cassie narrowed her eyes. "I bet Devin would remember."

"He might. I'm actually surprised the place hasn't closed down, yet. Before Emma started working there, I heard rumors that it had huge debts and it was going to." Sebastian nodded then held out the glass to her. "If you don't mind I'll keep working for a little while."

"Let me help. I'll just put this inside and change into some jeans, I'll be right out." Cassie started for the back porch.

"Cassie, you don't have to do that." Sebastian

shook his head. "It's hot, and you don't want to get all dirty."

Cassie glanced back at him as she reached the porch and smiled.

"I don't mind a little dirt." She hurried into the house and quickly changed into more comfortable clothes. As she headed back outside, her cell phone buzzed with a text from Tessa.

Spoke to my contact. Emma's alibi verified. She was with Janice.

Cassie sighed with relief. She never wanted to believe that Emma was the murderer.

Her phone beeped with another text from Tessa.

She opened it to find a picture of a list of phone numbers.

Tessa also listed who the numbers belonged to. Emma, Aiden, and Adventures Aplenty, the company that Emma and Patrick worked for. After what she'd just learned from Sebastian, she decided it would be best to get in touch with Devin, the owner of Adventures Aplenty. She made the call and left a message requesting a tour of the facility. As she joined Sebastian in the backyard again, he pulled his shirt back on and she focused on digging into the soil.

"I'm sure you didn't do this too much living in the city." Sebastian glanced over at her.

"We did have a garden." Cassie smiled some as she recalled it. "My husband and I would tend it."

Cassie's words hung in the air between them.

"It must be hard." Sebastian let the shovel rest against his shoulder as he looked into her eyes. "Being here without him."

"Not really." Cassie caught her mistake as a flash of surprise crossed Sebastian's features. "I mean, I'm used to it now." Guilt rushed through her.

"Cassie, you don't have to explain yourself to me." Sebastian took the shovel from her hand as he lowered his voice. "Not all marriages are happy."

Cassie froze as his words cut through the mask she'd been wearing for so long. Her stomach twisted as he spoke about something that she'd been doing her best to avoid. Although she missed her husband, they had grown apart in recent years. His unexpected death in a car accident had come as a shock to her and although she wished it had never happened and he was still in her life, she was ready to move forward.

"It's complicated." She released the breath she'd been holding.

"You don't have to tell me anything." Sebastian

brushed some dirt from her cheek and shook his head. "I just want you to know, I'm here to listen, if you ever want to talk."

"Thanks Sebastian." Cassie found comfort in the genuine warmth that encapsulated his voice. She'd been so frightened to admit the truth about her marriage, but somehow he'd picked up on her feelings, despite her attempt to hide them, even from herself.

CHAPTER 23

"We better get to it." Cassie smiled at Sebastian as she gestured to her garden.

"Am I interrupting?" Oliver's voice called out from near the back porch.

Cassie swung around so fast that she caught her foot on one of the shovels that Sebastian held, which made the handle smack into his cheek.

"Ouch!" He winced and laughed at the same time.

"Oh, Sebastian, I'm so sorry!" Cassie gasped as she turned back to face him.

"Don't worry about it." Sebastian waved his hand then nodded to Oliver. "We're just working on the garden. It looks like you have some news?"

"I do." Oliver stared hard at Sebastian, then

turned his attention to Cassie. "I wanted to let you know that Clyde's death has officially been declared a homicide, and I have made an arrest."

"What?" Cassie's eyes widened. "How? Who?" Her heart raced at the thought of it all being over.

"We were able to confirm that the ring you found at the campsite belongs to Ron, and he has been arrested for Clyde's murder. I asked the medical examiner to check again for any other indication of foul play on Clyde's body, and she found some contusions that had yet to surface at the time of the murder and initial examination. It looks like Clyde and Ron had a run-in, and Ron must have knocked him out. My guess is that he assumed he was dead." Oliver frowned.

"But he wasn't?" Sebastian stepped up beside Cassie.

"No. It was the stove that killed him, the medical examiner was right, but there hadn't been any indication of a fight before. Once we discovered that, and that the ring belonged to Ron, we were able to solve the case." Oliver paused as he shook his head. "Clyde even had some of Ron's DNA on him."

"I guess that's that, then." Cassie shrugged. "I wonder how Trevor is taking it."

"I'm not sure that he knows, yet." Oliver frowned

as he glanced up at her. "I thought maybe you would like to tell him. I'm not sure he would take it well coming from me."

"Not likely." Sebastian set the shovels he held down on the ground. "I'm sure we can find him."

"Thanks for the update, Oliver." Cassie's mind still swam as she tried to piece Ron's actions together. Did he admit to it? Why did they fight? Was it because he was jealous over Clyde's relationship with Trevor? Was it because of the way he treated Trevor's mother? Trevor had mentioned that Clyde argued with Ron over it. It was a long time ago, but some things took time to forget. "Did he say anything else?"

"No, he's not saying a word. The moment we put handcuffs on him, he asked for a lawyer. But I'm sure once he sees the evidence against him he'll want to plead guilty to reduce his charges." Oliver cleared his throat. "Cassie, could I speak to you for a moment about our plans?"

"Sure." Cassie shifted from one foot to the other as Sebastian looked over at her.

"I thought perhaps we could move them to tonight, since the case is closed now." Oliver looked into her eyes. "Would that be alright with you?"

"Great." Cassie willed her face not to feel so hot

as she felt the attention of both men on her. She couldn't turn him down in front of Sebastian, she might embarrass him. Instead, she felt forced to affirm that she would have dinner with him, when her instincts told her she needed to do everything she could to get out of it.

"Okay, good." Oliver smiled awkwardly. "I'll text you later then."

"Perfect." Cassie forced the word out, then stood completely still as Oliver left the yard.

"Plans, huh?" Sebastian's voice lightened with a hint of amusement.

"I should go find Trevor." Cassie avoided looking in his direction.

"I'll finish up here." Sebastian grabbed one of the shovels from the ground. "Unless you want me to come with."

"That's okay. I'll be fine." As Cassie started toward the front yard, he called after her.

"Be careful with Trevor, Cassie, he can be a loose cannon."

"I will be, thanks. Call me if you need me." Again, she refused to look in his direction. How could things get more uncomfortable? She heard the shovel slide into the dirt behind her. It didn't seem to bother him at all that she had plans with Oliver. Maybe Tessa was wrong, maybe Sebastian didn't have an interest in her after all. Cassie expected to be relieved by that thought. Instead she felt a subtle tug of disappointment.

It didn't take her long to find Trevor in the alley where he usually worked on his art. She expected to discover him wrapped up in a new creation. Instead, she found him sitting on the ground with his phone in his hand.

"Trevor?" Cassie paused a few feet away from him.

"What?" Trevor didn't look up at her. Instead, he continued to scroll through his phone.

Cassie crouched down beside him and tried to catch his eye. "Trevor, have you heard what's happened?"

"You mean, have I heard that my father is a murderer?" Trevor looked up at her then, his eyes hard and his voice hot with anger.

"Yes." Cassie edged back some as she wondered just how much of a loose cannon Trevor could be. She'd known him to be a passionate artist, but he was still quite young, and had a tendency to get into trouble.

"Yup, I've heard, I'm making plans to celebrate

right now." Trevor smiled as he shook his head. "My mom will be thrilled."

"I'm not sure that's true, Trevor." Cassie straightened up as she looked down at him. "It's okay to feel upset by all of this, you know? I'm sure it's quite a shock."

"A shock?" Trevor stood up as well. "No, it's not a shock. I've known he was a loser for most of my life."

"There's a difference between being a loser, and being a murderer." Cassie looked into his eyes. "You don't have to play tough with me, Trevor."

"Play tough?" Trevor stepped back. "I'm not playing, Cassie. Not at all. I'm just glad it's all finally over."

"I'm sorry, Trevor. You lost someone you cared about, and now you're faced with the fact that your father is the cause. I want to make sure you're okay." Cassie searched his eyes. "If you won't talk to me, is there someone you will talk to? Maybe Sebastian?"

"Cassie, don't." Trevor looked away from her.

"I'm not trying to make things harder on you. I'm really not." Cassie watched his cheeks redden. "At least you can take some comfort knowing that Clyde's murder has been solved."

"There it is!" Trevor snapped at her as he slammed his hand against the dumpster beside him.

Cassie jumped in reaction to the loud sound he created and the sudden shift in his tone.

"Trevor?" She moved back some as he glared at her. "I was just trying to help, but if you'd rather be alone I can go."

"I'd rather just be able to take this as a win." Trevor curled his hands into fists. "I'd rather be able to leave my father to rot in jail. It's where he deserves to be!"

"What do you mean?" Cassie narrowed her eyes.

"I mean, Clyde's murder hasn't been solved, Cassie!"

CHAPTER 24

"What do you mean, Clyde's murder hasn't been solved?" Cassie stared straight at Trevor.

"I don't want to talk about it! Okay?" Trevor threw his hands into the air. "I just want to leave it alone."

"Trevor!" Cassie stepped around him so she was facing him. She was no longer intimidated by his outbursts. She was determined to get to the truth. "You listen to me. If you know something about your father's involvement in Clyde's murder, then you absolutely have to tell the truth!"

"Do I?" Trevor glared at her. "Why do I have to tell the truth when he never stops lying? Isn't it funny?" He laughed as he looked up at the sky, then back at her. "The police think he cares enough about me to murder someone? Yeah right. He barely knows that I exist."

"But your father's ring was found at the campsite. Clyde had his DNA on him." Cassie shook her head. "I know this can be hard to take in, Trevor, but the evidence shows that your father did murder Clyde."

"No, it shows that he did get into a fistfight with Clyde. Which I know he did." Trevor crossed his arms and sighed. "He told me last night. He was drunk, and thought that Aiden was me on the video. Can you believe that? He couldn't even tell us apart. He went up to the campsite to talk to me and got into a fight with Clyde. My guess is Clyde called him out on being an idiot and dear old Dad didn't like that." He crossed his arms. "So yeah, he and Clyde got into a bit of a fight, but Clyde was alive when he left there."

"How do you know that?" Cassie stared hard into his eyes. "How can you be sure?"

"I can be sure because Mom found him sleeping it off in our backyard before Clyde was killed." Trevor frowned. "She was covering for him as usual and didn't want to tell the police that he was drunk or had been in a fight, so she let him clean up and pretend it never happened. He told me last night because he realized he had lost his ring and thought it might be near where Clyde's body was found." He paused and took a deep breath. "He wanted me to know that he didn't kill Clyde. I guess, he was worried about what I would think of him."

"But he's been arrested now. Why isn't your mother telling the police about your father's alibi?" Cassie frowned.

"Because she doesn't know that he's been arrested. She's away on a trip with her friend and she won't be back until tomorrow. I don't know if there's no cell reception or her phone is just off, but her phone is going straight to voicemail. I'm sure my dad has no idea where she is or how to get in contact with her." Trevor shrugged. "So, I figured I'd let him sit in there. I mean, just because he concocted some story with my mother doesn't make him innocent, right? Maybe it's just her trying to cover up for him again."

"Trevor, you don't really believe that, do you?" Cassie realized that Oliver's closed case had just been broken wide open again.

"No." Trevor closed his eyes. "No, I don't believe he did it. But so what?" He opened his eyes again.

"You don't really believe that he should be in jail if he's innocent, do you? You know what the problem is, Trevor. Every moment they spend thinking that your father did this, is another minute they're not finding Clyde's real killer. I can understand why you want to get some revenge on your father, but is that fair to Clyde? Do you think it's right for his killer to go free just so you can settle a score with your father?"

"See, I knew you would ruin it." Trevor groaned, then smacked his hand against his thigh. "Just like usual, I get stuck doing the dirty work because of him. What do you think Oliver is going to do to me when he finds out I've been holding out and wasting his time?"

"Don't worry about Oliver." Cassie smiled. "I'll talk to him about it first. You just try to get in contact with your mother, because Oliver is going to want to confirm your father's alibi."

"I'll do my best." Trevor pulled out his phone, then looked over at her. "Thanks Cassie."

"Good luck with your mom." Cassie headed back down the alley. Then she drove straight to the police station. If what Trevor said was true, then Oliver needed to know right away, before he lost more precious time. Her mind swirled as she realized this meant that all of the suspects were in play again. If Ron didn't kill Clyde, then who did?

"Oliver!" Cassie spotted him just inside the doors of the police station.

"Cassie? Is everything okay?" Oliver walked over to her, his eyes narrowed.

"I just spoke with Trevor. Ron has an alibi for the time of Clyde's death." Cassie rushed through the explanation that Trevor had given her.

"Cassie, are you sure that isn't just a son trying to cover up for his father?" Oliver shook his head. "It's not exactly a solid alibi, considering the evidence we have, I'd say he's still our prime suspect."

"Once Trevor gets in contact with his mother, she can confirm the alibi." Cassie frowned. "I just didn't want you to think that you have the murderer in custody."

"As of now, I do." Oliver shrugged. "Until I receive some evidence that proves otherwise. But I will begin reviewing the other suspects again. Thanks for the information, Cassie."

"You're not going to release him?" Cassie sighed, even though she expected that would be the case.

"I can't do that without cause. As soon as I am able to confirm his alibi I will move forward from there." Oliver started down the hallway in the direction of his desk, then paused. "We're still on for tonight, right?"

"Yes, sure." Cassie knew that Oliver had to follow the rules, but she couldn't help but wonder if an innocent man might stay behind bars while a killer roamed free.

Cassie continued to dwell on that possibility as she drove back to her house. She noticed right away that Sebastian's truck was gone.

"That's for the best." She frowned as she stepped out of the car. She couldn't just do nothing. She needed to try and help find out who had killed Clyde.

As Cassie paced through her kitchen, she ran through the suspects in her mind. Even if she eliminated Ron as a suspect there were still several other possibilities. Aiden, Justin, Patrick or Shane, even the two criminals on the run, were still options.

Cassie's phone buzzed in her pocket. She pulled it out and saw a message from Oliver with the time and restaurant for that evening. One of the few restaurants in Little Leaf Creek, a small pizza place.

Cassie stared at the text on her screen and wondered if she should reply. She could just pretend she hadn't received it. But didn't police detectives have a way of checking into those kinds of things? She sighed and closed her eyes. She didn't think that Oliver would ever invade her privacy that way, but the truth was, she didn't know him that well. She assumed he wanted to change that, by getting to know each other a little better. But was she really ready for that? She recalled what Tessa said about Oliver's serious nature when it came to relationships. She couldn't string him along, not even about a first date.

As Cassie set her phone down, she had to admit that she felt a tiny burst of excitement at his interest.

The buzz of her cell phone made her jump. She snatched it up, thinking it was another text from Oliver. Instead, it was a text from Devin. The owner of Adventures Aplenty. The place where Emma and her brother, Patrick, worked.

"Finally, he got back to me." Cassie smiled as she read the message, glad that he had agreed to give her a tour of his facility. It would be the perfect chance to find out more about the fight between Justin and Clyde that he had witnessed. Maybe it would be the break in the case that she needed. It also gave her a good excuse not to think about Oliver for the next hour or so. She sent a quick text back letting Devin know that she was on her way, then sent a text to Oliver assuring him that she would meet him for dinner. One of two things would happen, either she would decide to see where things went with him, or she would find a way to stop the whole thing from progressing. Either way she had to face it.

CHAPTER 25

On the drive to Adventures Aplenty, Cassie tried to piece together the questions she wanted to ask Devin. He had not only witnessed the fight, but he had worked with Patrick and Emma for some time, and he also knew of Clyde. She guessed that the best way to find out what he thought about Clyde's murder and his murderer was to find out what he thought of Clyde himself.

Cassie parked in the empty parking lot and headed for the front door. She noted that the hours on the door indicated that Adventures Aplenty had already closed for the day. She gave a light knock on the door and peered inside. Maybe she had read the message wrong? She was just about to pull her phone out to check when she heard someone walking toward the door.

Cassie was surprised to see Emma open the door.

"Cassie!" Emma smiled broadly.

"Emma, it's so nice to see you." Cassie smiled in return.

"Oh, it's nice to see you again, too. Come inside." Emma held the door open and gestured for Cassie to step inside. "Devin said he had arranged to give you a tour, but something came up, so he asked for me to do it." She started guiding her down a corridor.

"Thank you." Cassie felt a bit disappointed. She had wanted to speak to Devin, but it was still another opportunity to speak to Emma. "It's great that he's letting me take this tour."

"Devin is always eager to find a new customer." Emma smiled. "I'm surprised you're interested in climbing. Have you ever climbed before?"

"I haven't. But I'd like to learn."

"Come, let me show you around." Emma began to lead her through the large space.

"This is a nice place to work." Cassie looked up at the zipline that ran through the largest part of the building, then disappeared around a corner. "I bet you have a lot of people interested in your packages."

"We do, we do." Emma smiled. "Once people try

it out, they love it. You know some people, they want the elements, the rugged mountains, the freezing ski slopes, but others like their adventure to be a little bit more controlled. That's what this place offers. All of the adventure with very little risk." She pointed up at cameras mounted on the ceiling. "Everything is monitored, and as a bonus, customers can choose to take home videos of all of their activities."

"Great idea." Cassie smiled as she followed along behind her. "Did Clyde ever come here?"

"Clyde." Emma placed her hand on her chest and sighed. "Yes, he was here once. It was before we met and I didn't work here yet, but he told me all about his visit. He wasn't terribly impressed. He's a bit of a purist when it comes to adventure. But not everyone wants the wind in their hair or a rainstorm to force them into a cave. Predictability may change adventure, but it doesn't negate it." She paused near a rock climbing wall. "I've seen people just as thrilled when they reach the top of this wall, as I've seen people thrilled on a regular mountain climb. Of course we still offer outdoor adventures, too. We cover all of the bases here."

"It looks like a lot of time has been spent building up this business." Cassie looked around the large room.

"And a lot of money." Emma shook her head. "But it's worth it for all the adventure."

"I'm sure it is." Cassie looked up at the top of the wall that towered over her. "Sounds great."

"It's so exhilarating. It's so much fun." Emma pointed toward the wall. "Why don't you have a try?"

"Now, oh no I can't do that." Cassie looked back at her.

"Come on, it will be fun." Emma grabbed some ropes. The excitement in her eyes made Cassie enthusiastic.

"Okay." Cassie laughed. "Why not." She thought about the promise to herself that she didn't want to miss out on things in life, and rock climbing would definitely be an adventure.

"Exactly." Emma wrapped the ropes around Cassie's waist. "It's easy, trust me."

"I'm so sorry. This is such a difficult time for you. You must miss Clyde." Cassie looked into her eyes

"I can't miss someone like him." Emma's voice turned cold. "He betrayed me. He needed to be eliminated."

"Eliminated?" Cassie gasped. Before she knew what was happening Emma tied some ropes around her arms. "Why? What are you doing?" She looked at her arms.

"Clyde was going to ruin everything." Emma scowled.

"What?" Cassie's eyes widened. She couldn't comprehend what was happening. Did Emma really kill Clyde?

"You see, I am a partner in Adventures Aplenty. I worked so hard on the business. I worked so hard to make it a success. Devin was losing money and he offered me a share of the business to save it. I poured my life-savings into the place to save it and make it a success." Emma scowled. "Which is why, when I found out Clyde was going to start his own adventure business I did whatever I could to stop him. I tried to convince him that it was a bad idea."

"You tried to stop him from getting the permits?" Cassie scowled.

"Yep, it was me." Emma smiled.

"But you cared about him."

"Nope, I used him. I asked him if he would let me be his partner in his new endeavor and he just brushed me off. He wanted to set up the business with Shane. I only went out with him to try and get information out of him about what he was planning with the business. I couldn't let his plans ruin me."

"It's just a business. How could you kill him for that?"

"I had nothing. We had nothing. Patrick and me. I have worked so hard to make sure I get everything I need in life. To make sure Patrick gets everything he needs in life." Emma shook her head. "I did what I did so we didn't lose our jobs, and I didn't lose my business."

As Cassie stood there tied up, she realized now that she'd put herself in a terrible position. She was alone in a large, empty building with a woman she now was certain was a killer. She had never truly believed that Emma could be the one to kill Clyde. She could never believe that she would lure her there. But obviously she had been wrong.

"And you thought killing Clyde would help you?" Cassie frowned. Maybe if she got her to talk long enough, someone would magically show up to help her. But she had no idea who that could be.

"I didn't mean to kill Clyde. But once I did, I had to cover my tracks. Now I have to take care of you." Emma scowled.

"But you didn't kill Clyde. He was just knocked out. The stove killed him." Cassie shook her head.

"I know that now. But I panicked, I thought I had killed him when he wasn't moving so I tried to cover it up. But I won't be that sloppy again." Emma pointed to the wall behind Cassie. "Start climbing.

You came here for an adventure, right? So, now you're going to have one. It will just be another tragic accident. An inexperienced climber who decided to climb unsupervised, and slipped."

"No one will believe that!" Cassie thrashed against the ropes.

"They'll believe what I tell them to believe. Now, start climbing, or I can make things much worse for you." Emma scowled up at her.

"I won't!" Cassie struggled to get free of the rope that Emma had tightened around her waist.

"You will." Emma nodded. "This is all your fault. You decided to dig too deep and try to solve this. All you had to do was let it go."

"How could you kill him just because he wanted to open an adventure tourism business?" Cassie tried to keep her breathing even.

"Just because?" Emma laughed. "I didn't even mean to kill him. I just wanted to talk. He had arranged for me to go climbing with him instead of Aiden. It was supposed to be some fun. I thought one last bit of adventure with Clyde before I broke up with him. You see, I had achieved my goal. I knew about the fight between Shane and him and that the business was over. But when I came to the campsite, he was in a bad mood. He had already been fighting with Ron. When he told me that the fight between Shane and him was faked, I lost it. We were inside his tent and I pushed him. He fell back and he wasn't moving. I thought he was dead. I knew this was my only opportunity to protect myself."

"So, you tried to make it look like an accident?" Cassie tried to keep her voice steady.

"I did. I panicked." Emma glared at her. "I couldn't throw him off the cliff, it was too hard to drag him so far. The stove was right there. I had to do something to try and cover my tracks. I had no other choice." Emma sighed. "But when I calmed down I realized that no one would believe that Clyde would have that stove in his tent. At least no one who knew Clyde. So, I had to tell Oliver that I believed it was a murder and try to help him, otherwise he might have been suspicious of me."

"You planned all of this?" Cassie tugged on the rope that tied her arms. It was tied too tightly and she couldn't get a grip on it. "You lured me here."

"You thought you were so clever with that little ruse you came up with. But when Devin said you had called for a tour, I knew you were up to something. Then after you spoke to Patrick, I knew you were getting real close. So, I decided to let you walk right into my trap." Emma pulled hard on the rope that fed through the other side of the pulley. Cassie shrieked, as her body was yanked up off the ground and launched into the air.

"Stop!" Cassie waved her hands through the air in an attempt to grab onto anything that would keep her from slamming back down into the ground.

"Hang on a second." Emma tied the rope off and stared up at her. "I don't want you making a mess of the floor. Too much trouble to clean it." She turned and walked off.

Desperate, Cassie tugged at the rope wrapped around her. When it began to slide a little she realized that she would just plummet to the ground without it. She swung her feet in an attempt to reach the rock wall. If she could at least grab onto something she might be able to climb. However, she'd never climbed a rock wall in her life, and she doubted that she would be able to start now. She had to get help somehow. Her purse had fallen to the ground when Emma had pulled her up the wall, but her phone was in her pocket. With the way the rope was tied around her she couldn't quite reach it. She twisted her hips and wriggled in an attempt to get her finger hooked into her pocket.

"Like a fish on a line." Emma chuckled as she walked back toward her with a large plastic sheet.

"I'll just tell them I planned to do some touch-ups. It'll just be a happy coincidence that I won't have to scrape your remains off the floor."

"You're not going to get away with this, Emma! You haven't thought this through! I'm supposed to be having dinner with Oliver right now. He's going to start looking for me the moment that I don't show up. You might kill me, but he'll never believe that I stood him up to go rock climbing!"

"Oh, is that so?" Emma flashed her a grin as she picked up Cassie's purse. "I guess I'm just going to have to make sure he believes me then." She emptied the contents of her purse, then frowned. "Where's your phone?" She swept her gaze along Cassie's jeans, then shook her head. "I can see it in your pocket." She untied the rope and lowered her enough that she could reach her, then tied it again.

As Emma leaned in to fish out her phone, Cassie swung her leg as hard as she could toward her.

Emma jumped out of the way just before her leg connected with her.

"Feisty, aren't you? I can see why Sebastian likes you." Emma chuckled. "Nice try, but you're not getting away from me." She began to type out a message on her phone. "Sorry Oliver, will have to postpone dinner, I need to do some rock climbing."

Emma grinned as she looked up at her. "Now, who is he going to believe?"

"Don't bother sending it, he's not going to believe it. He knows I would never cancel dinner with him." Cassie's heart pounded as she knew otherwise. Oliver wouldn't be surprised if she canceled. But she hoped the text would be enough to arouse his suspicions, and make him wonder whether she might be in trouble.

"Too late, I already sent it." Emma began to hike her high up toward the ceiling again. "Don't worry, they say it's exhilarating until you hit the ground."

Cassie held her breath as she braced herself for the fall.

A knock on the door made Emma huff with annoyance. "Hate to leave you hanging, but I'd better see what that's about." She tied the rope again, which left Cassie suspended high in the air. Then Emma walked off toward the door.

Knowing this might be her only chance, Cassie swung herself as hard as she could toward the rock wall. As her fingertips grazed the surface, her body swung back in the other direction. Tears stung her eyes as she realized how futile it was. Still, she continued to try.

If someone was at the front door they might be able to hear her. She shouted as loud as she could.

"Help! Please help me!" Cassie shrieked until her throat ached. Out of breath, she stopped for a few seconds.

Footsteps. In the absence of her scream, she heard footsteps walking in her direction. Her heart raced as she wondered if it might be someone coming to save her. But the closer the footsteps came, the less hope she held onto. They weren't quick. Each step was delivered at an even, casual pace.

"Tired yourself out a bit, did you?" Emma smiled as she stepped into her line of sight. "All of that thrashing and screaming was really unnecessary. You see, this area of the building is soundproofed. It keeps the distractions out, and the music that people enjoy listening to while they climb, in." She crossed her arms as she stared up at her. "That was Patrick by the way. He decided to come back to make sure I was okay and I didn't need help with your tour. He was worried you would question me about Clyde and upset me. Isn't it funny the things that people worry about? He's always trying to make sure I am okay. If only he knew how I can take care of myself." She chuckled. "I assured him that I am fine." She walked over to the rope and dusted off her hands. "Now, where were we?"

"Please!" The word sounded strange, as Cassie's throat still throbbed from screaming. "Please just let me go, Emma. I know you don't really want to do this. Clyde was going to ruin your future, but I won't do that. I'm just here by mistake, that's all. If you let me go, I won't tell anyone!"

"Oh, I'm going to let you go alright." Emma grinned as she began to unwind the rope.

"Emma, don't!" Cassie swung her legs wildly. "Please!"

"Enough!" Emma whipped the rope free and let it slide out of her hands. As it made its way through the pulley, she turned and walked away.

Cassie gasped as her body jolted, then began to descend.

CHAPTER 26

Cassie felt the rush of the fall as her body plunged toward the floor. As she braced herself for the pain, a part of her hoped that it would be quick. She squeezed her eyes shut and held her breath. When she suddenly jerked to a stop, she realized tears had begun sliding down her cheeks.

"Cassie!" Oliver shouted from below her. He looked up at her, his cheeks flushed, his mouth half-open, and his hands wrapped tightly around the rope that held her in place.

"Oliver!" Cassie cried out as she wondered if she was imagining his presence. "Oliver, don't let go!"

"I'm not going to." Oliver eased the rope slowly through the pulley, bringing her closer to the ground. "Easy now, almost there."

Cassie shuddered as her shoes scraped the floor. Oliver released the rope, then rushed to her side just in time for her to collapse into his arms. Tears continued to flow down her cheeks as she wrapped her arms around him and clung so tight that her arms trembled.

"It's okay, Cassie, you're safe now," Oliver murmured. "I've got you."

Cassie took a breath as she pulled away from him, still shaking from the adrenaline that coursed through her.

"It's Emma! Did you catch her?"

"Yes, officers caught her coming out the door, I came in here to find you." Oliver's breath caught in his throat as he stared at her.

"Just in time." Cassie gazed at him. "How?"

"After you told me about Ron having an alibi. I dug back into the suspects that I'd been looking into before I arrested Ron." Oliver shook his head. "I'm sorry I didn't get here sooner."

"Then it wasn't the text?" Cassie wiped the tears from her cheeks.

"I didn't get any text." Oliver began to loosen the ropes from around her body. "Are you hurt?"

"No." Cassie breathed a sigh of relief. "I'm okay.

I'm just so glad you figured it all out. I never really thought that Emma could be the killer. I still can't believe she could be. Apparently, she pushed Clyde and he hit his head. She thought he was dead. So, she placed the stove in his tent to cover her tracks. How did you know to come here?"

"I had been reviewing the business' financial statements. I noticed how tenuous they were, up until a few months ago. Before Emma started working there. Then shortly after she started working there, money started being injected into the business. Not much, but enough to keep it afloat. It was around the same time that Emma was listed as a partner in the business. I spoke to Devin and he said that Emma had invested in the business when it was about to go under. She had saved his business. He admitted that she was the ringleader in trying to ensure that Clyde and Shane's business never got off the ground. I then spoke to Aiden again and he finally admitted that he thought Clyde had ditched him to see Emma."

"Poor Sebastian." Cassie sighed. "He is going to feel terrible about this."

"Actually, Sebastian helped the final pieces fall into place. He said that he ran into Emma's friend,

Janice, the one that said she was with her when Clyde was killed. She admitted to Sebastian that she had lied, and that she had only spent a bit of time with Emma that night. Emma had asked Janice to cover for her so she wouldn't get into trouble with Patrick for seeing Clyde. Then Emma told Janice to tell the police the same story so Patrick wouldn't get angry with Emma for lying to him. Janice felt bad about lying and wanted to tell someone the truth. When Sebastian heard what Emma asked Janice to do, he suspected something was wrong. He knew that Emma had time to go up to the campsite and kill Clyde. He called her to ask about it and he said she sounded weird. She was evasive and she contradicted herself. He just really didn't want to believe she was involved, and neither did I. But he called me to tell me what he had learned so I could look into it properly."

"He must have been really suspicious to call you."

"He was, he kept saying that he couldn't believe she would do this, but something was wrong. When I went to speak to Emma at her house, Patrick was there and he said that she was still at work. I came here because I wanted to speak to her." Oliver took her hand. "But I had no idea you were here until I saw your car in the parking lot. Then I knew, you might be in danger." He looked away from her. "When I saw you falling, I just—" His voice cracked as he clenched his jaw.

"It's okay." Cassie squeezed his hand. "I'm okay. Thanks to you."

"You should get checked out by the medics just in case. You're running on adrenaline and may not feel any injuries right now." Oliver gazed down at the plastic they stood on. "I can't believe she planned all of this out. I started suspecting Emma, but I had no idea that she had this in her."

"I never really thought she could have done this." Cassie continued to cling to his hand as he led her through the building, and out into the sunlight.

"She's going to pay for what she did to Clyde, and what she did to you." Oliver glared at Emma as officers guided her into a patrol car.

"Thank you, Oliver." Cassie squeezed his hand as she looked into his eyes, and watched them soften with warmth. "I was so scared hanging from that wall. I was sure I was going to die."

"But you didn't." Oliver smiled. "Now you can see what the future holds for you in Little Leaf Creek."

"Yes, you're right." Cassie took a deep breath of the fresh air and felt the fear and adrenaline that had been pulsing through her veins since Emma grabbed her, begin to ease. "Starting with dinner tonight?"

"I don't think so." Oliver turned away as an officer called out to him. When he looked back at her, his stern expression had returned. "When we go out, it's going to be on a night that neither of us is distracted. Tonight, after you're checked out, you need to rest. I'll check on you later."

Though Cassie felt a hint of disappointment at their date being canceled, she couldn't deny that his concern for her made warmth well up inside of her. He'd been there when she needed him the most, and now, he wanted to be sure that she was okay.

As the medics looked her over, Cassie watched Oliver speak to the gathered officers. What she had once seen as sternness, she now saw as determination and attention to detail. If he hadn't noticed her car in the parking lot, if he hadn't already suspected Emma as the killer, she wouldn't be getting poked and prodded by medics. She would probably be dead.

Oliver glanced back at her and caught her eye. His lips spread into a reassuring smile, then he turned back to the other officers. It was in that moment that she began to look forward to going out with him. She didn't know where it might lead, but she wanted to find out. Once she was given the all clear by the medics, she began to walk back toward her car. Before she could reach it, she felt something wet and warm against the palm of her hand.

"Harry!" Cassie laughed, as she pulled her hand away from the lapping of the dog's tongue. There wasn't much that could bring a smile to her face after what she had just been through, but Harry's presence did it. "Where did you come from?"

"Oliver called me." Tessa walked up beside her. "He wants me to make sure that you get home safe." She placed her hand on her shoulder and looked into her eyes. "Are you okay?"

"I'm fine." Cassie glanced over at Oliver, then looked back at Tessa with a faint smile. "Thanks to Oliver. I can't believe he called you." She turned back to face her. "See? You two are going to reconnect."

"We'll just have to see, won't we." Tessa lifted her hand in a light wave to Oliver.

Oliver stared at her for a long moment, then nodded.

"See, progress." Cassie looped her arm around Tessa's.

"It's a nod, Cassie." Tessa chuckled as she walked her toward her jeep.

"It's a start." Cassie took a deep breath. It was a

start for Tessa and Oliver, but it was also a start for her. Little Leaf Creek was her chance to put the past behind her, and although things hadn't gone as she planned, she was ready to see where the new start would lead next.

The End

ABOUT THE AUTHOR

Cindy Bell is a USA Today and Wall Street Journal Bestselling Author. She is the author of the Little Leaf Creek, Wagging Tail, Donut Truck, Dune House, Sage Gardens, Chocolate Centered, Macaron Patisserie, Nuts about Nuts, Bekki the Beautician, Heavenly Highland Inn and Wendy the Wedding Planner cozy mystery series.

Cindy has always loved reading, but it is only recently that she has discovered her passion for writing romantic cozy mysteries. She loves walking along the beach thinking of the next adventure her characters can embark on.

You can sign up for her newsletter so you are notified of her latest releases at http://www.cindybellbooks.com.

ALSO BY CINDY BELL

LITTLE LEAF CREEK COZY MYSTERY SERIES

Chaos in Little Leaf Creek

CHOCOLATE CENTERED COZY MYSTERIES

The Sweet Smell of Murder

A Deadly Delicious Delivery

A Bitter Sweet Murder

A Treacherous Tasty Trail

Pastry and Peril

Trouble and Treats

Fudge Films and Felonies

Custom-Made Murder

Skydiving, Soufflés and Sabotage

Christmas Chocolates and Crimes

Hot Chocolate and Homicide

Chocolate Caramels and Conmen

Picnics, Pies and Lies

Devils Food Cake and Drama

Cinnamon and a Corpse

Cherries, Berries and a Body

Christmas Cookies and Criminals

Grapes, Ganache & Guilt

DUNE HOUSE COZY MYSTERIES

Seaside Secrets

Boats and Bad Guys

Treasured History

Hidden Hideaways

Dodgy Dealings

Suspects and Surprises

Ruffled Feathers

A Fishy Discovery

Danger in the Depths

Celebrities and Chaos

Pups, Pilots and Peril

Tides, Trails and Trouble

Racing and Robberies

Athletes and Alibis

Manuscripts and Deadly Motives

Pelicans, Pier and Poison

Sand, Sea and a Skeleton

Pianos and Prison

WAGGING TAIL COZY MYSTERIES

Murder at Pawprint Creek (prequel)

Murder at Pooch Park

Murder at the Pet Boutique

A Merry Murder at St. Bernard Cabins

Murder at the Dog Training Academy

Murder at Corgi Country Club

A Merry Murder on Ruff Road

Murder at Poodle Place

Murder at Hound Hill

Murder at Rover Meadows

SAGE GARDENS COZY MYSTERIES

Sage Gardens Cozy Mystery Series Box Set Volume 1 (Books 1 - 4)

Birthdays Can Be Deadly

Money Can Be Deadly

Trust Can Be Deadly

Ties Can Be Deadly

Rocks Can Be Deadly

Jewelry Can Be Deadly

Numbers Can Be Deadly

Memories Can Be Deadly

Paintings Can Be Deadly

Snow Can Be Deadly

Tea Can Be Deadly

Greed Can Be Deadly

Clutter Can Be Deadly

NUTS ABOUT NUTS COZY MYSTERIES

A Tough Case to Crack

A Seed of Doubt

Roasted Peanuts and Peril

Chestnuts, Camping and Culprits

DONUT TRUCK COZY MYSTERIES

Deadly Deals and Donuts

Fatal Festive Donuts

Bunny Donuts and a Body

Strawberry Donuts and Scandal

Frosted Donuts and Fatal Falls

BEKKI THE BEAUTICIAN COZY MYSTERIES

Hairspray and Homicide

A Dyed Blonde and a Dead Body

Mascara and Murder

Pageant and Poison

Conditioner and a Corpse

Mistletoe, Makeup and Murder

Hairpin, Hair Dryer and Homicide

Blush, a Bride and a Body

Shampoo and a Stiff

Cosmetics, a Cruise and a Killer

Lipstick, a Long Iron and Lifeless

Camping, Concealer and Criminals

Treated and Dyed

A Wrinkle-Free Murder

A MACARON PATISSERIE COZY MYSTERY SERIES

Sifting for Suspects

Recipes and Revenge

Mansions, Macarons and Murder

HEAVENLY HIGHLAND INN COZY MYSTERIES

Murdering the Roses

Dead in the Daisies

Killing the Carnations

Drowning the Daffodils

Suffocating the Sunflowers

Books, Bullets and Blooms

A Deadly Serious Gardening Contest

A Bridal Bouquet and a Body

Digging for Dirt

WENDY THE WEDDING PLANNER COZY MYSTERIES

Matrimony, Money and Murder

Chefs, Ceremonies and Crimes

Knives and Nuptials

Mice, Marriage and Murder

TESSA'S BAKED STRAWBERRY CHEESECAKE RECIPE

INGREDIENTS:

For the Crust

2 cups graham cracker crumbs (about 15 full graham crackers)
1/4 cup granulated sugar
5 tablespoons butter melted

For the Filling

4 packs (8oz) cream cheese at room temperature
1 1/4 cups granulated sugar
3/4 cup sour cream at room temperature

2 teaspoons vanilla extract
2 teaspoons fresh lemon juice
4 eggs at room temperature

For the Strawberry Topping

1 pound strawberries
1/3 cup granulated sugar
1 tablespoon fresh lemon juice

A few fresh strawberries to decorate (optional)

PREPARATION:

Preheat the oven to 350 degrees Fahrenheit. Place the oven rack in the bottom third of the oven. Wrap the outside of a 9 inch springform pan in heavy duty aluminum foil. Make sure it covers the base and sides of the pan. Do this 2 or 3 times to prevent water from seeping through the base of the pan into the cake as it will be baked in a water bath.

For the Crust

Using a food processor or a rolling pin and a bag

crush the graham crackers into crumbs. Place in a bowl and add the sugar and melted butter and mix together.

Place the mixture in the springform pan and compact it using a spoon or the underside of a cup. The mixture should cover the base and about three-quarters of the way up the sides of the pan.

Bake the cheesecake crust in the oven for 10 minutes. Take it out and leave it aside to cool while you make the filling.

For the Filling

Beat the cream cheese and sugar together.

Add the sour cream, vanilla extract and lemon juice and beat until well-combined.

Add the eggs one at a time, beating between each addition.

Beat until all the ingredients are mixed together, but don't overmix.

Pour the batter on top of the cooled crust and smooth the top with a spatula or knife.

Place the cake pan into a roasting dish and fill the dish with boiling water until it is about an inch up the side of the pan.

Place in the oven on the oven rack.

Bake in the pre-heated oven for 60 – 80 minutes. The cheesecake is ready when you shake the pan and there is no liquid but it still wobbles in the middle. When the cheesecake is ready, leave the oven door open about an inch and leave it in there for about an hour.

Take the cheesecake out of the oven and the roasting dish. With the cheesecake still in the springform pan place it on a wire rack to cool to room temperature. Then place in the refrigerator for at least 6 hours but preferably overnight.

After the cheesecake has been cooled in the refrigerator, make the strawberry topping.

For the Strawberry Topping

TESSA'S BAKED STRAWBERRY CHEESECAKE RECIPE

Hull and slice the strawberries into quarters. Put the strawberries, sugar and lemon juice in a medium saucepan. Place over medium heat until the mixture starts to boil. The juice will be released from the strawberries. Stir the mixture occasionally. Reduce the heat and simmer for about 18 – 24 minutes until the sauce is thickened. Put the mixture aside to cool.

Once cool, pour the strawberry topping over the top of the cheesecake and spread over the top. Place the fresh strawberries over the top to decorate. Remove the sides of the springform pan. Use a knife to pry the sides of the cake away from the pan if it is sticking anywhere.

When cutting the cake, place the knife in boiling water between cutting each piece so the cheesecake doesn't stick to the knife.

Enjoy!!